THE DONUT DIARIES

by Dermot Milligan

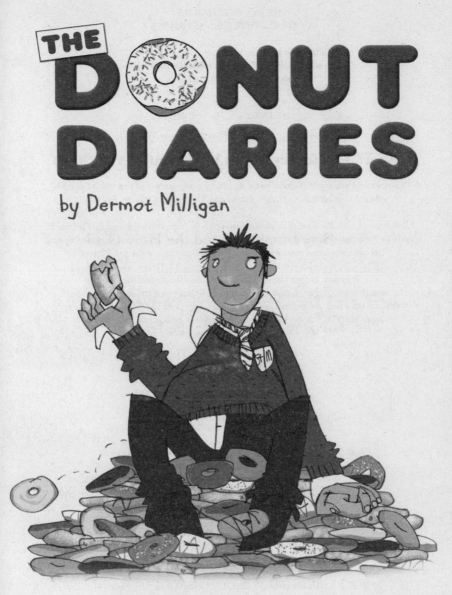

as told by Anthony McGowan

CORGI

THE DONUT DIARIES
A CORGI BOOK 978 0 552 56437 3

Published in Great Britain by Corgi Books,
an imprint of Random House Children's Books
A Random House Group Company

This edition published 2011

1 3 5 7 9 10 8 6 4 2

The Random House Group Limited supports the Forest Stewardship
Council® (FSC®), the leading international forest certification organiation.
All our titles that are printed on Greenpeace approved FSC® certified paper
carry the FSC® logo. Our paper procurement policy can be found at
www.randomhouse.co.uk/environment

Set in Bembo Regular 13pt/15.6pt

Corgi Books are published by Random House Children's Books,
61–63 Uxbridge Road, London W5 5SA

www.kidsatrandomhouse.co.uk
www.totallyrandombooks.co.uk
www.randomhouse.co.uk

Addresses for companies within The Random House Group Limited can be found at:
www.randomhouse.co.uk/offices.htm

THE RANDOM HOUSE GROUP Limited Reg. No. 954009

A CIP catalogue record for this book is available from the British Library.

Printed and bound in Great Britain by
CPI Bookmarque, Croydon, CRO 4TD

To Miss Eleanor Goldthorpe,

fairest of all the world's godchildren.

Tuesday 5 September

'No more arguments: either you see the nutritionist or you go to Camp Fatso in the next holiday.'

My mum could be pretty scary at times. Not zombie scary, but scary like thin ice over deep water.

We'd just watched the DVD that Camp Fatso had sent through the post. It's safe to say that the DVD is *not* aimed at the kids. It's most definitely aimed at the parents. We watched scenes of terrible torture. Fat kids are made to eat porridge in the morning. Then they are forced to run across miles of barren countryside, wearing vests and shorty shorts. Every five minutes they are compelled to lie on the ground and do press-ups.

For lunch there are leaves. Could be cabbage. Could be lettuce. Could be dandelion. But definitely leaves.

Then there is another cross-country run.

At dinner time the fat kids get fed stuff that looks a lot like the breakfast porridge, watered down.

From somewhere deep in my mind I realize that this stuff goes under the much feared name of 'gruel'.

No telly, no computers, no games consoles. For fun there is Snakes and Ladders and a jigsaw puzzle of some flowers.

The last scene shows the fat kids lying like corpses on beds so narrow their chubby butts flow out over the edges, like lava.

You know how in *The Lord of the Rings* the Balrog, with its Whip of Fire and really bad breath, is the one thing that Gandalf truly fears? Well, Camp Fatso was my Balrog.

'I AM NOT GOING THERE!' I said. 'NO WAY.'

It wasn't just the horror of the place – it was the stigma as well. What if word leaked out that I was at fat camp? It's the sort of thing that destroys your reputation for ever.

'Then you have to go and see the nutritionist,' said Mum. 'You'll like her. She's nice. I met her at my power yoga class.'

I looked at my dad. He'd come out of the toilet – where he spends most of his time –

specially to watch the DVD. He had a sorry,
pained expression on his face. It might have been
sympathy. It might have been wind. Either way,
there was no hope there. He wasn't going to
stand up to Mum.

So now you see why I was sitting in a room
that smelled faintly of puke. The puke smell was
partly covered over with pine air-freshener, but
only in the way that a kid might cover up his
mouth after saying a bad word.

Straight away the puke-and-pine combo
set off all kinds of scenes playing in my head,
most of them involving projectile vomiting
over Christmas trees. I guess that's the sort of
imagination I've got.

I'd just been weighed, prodded and poked,
with me wearing nothing but my boxer shorts,

so I wasn't in a great mood. If I'd known I was going to be standing there in nothing but my undies I'd have made sure they weren't my old T. Rex pants. Yep, that's a pair of underpants with a picture of a roaring T. Rex on them.

NOTE TO SELF: THROW AWAY, BURN, NUKE OR OTHERWISE UTTERLY DESTROY YOUR DINOSAUR PANTS BEFORE YOU START AT BIG SCHOOL ON MONDAY!!!!

'How many today, Dermot?'

The lady sitting in front of me smiled. It was the sort of smile that makes you wish you were holding a sharp stick, maybe with something smelly on the end of it. The sort of smelly thing that might recently have been inside a dog. But that's the sad thing about sharp sticks with something unpleasant on the end – you never seem to have one when you really need it.

'How many what?'

I said that, but I knew what she was talking about. I knew, and she knew that I knew. But she said it anyway, still smiling that horrible smile of hers.

'*Donuts,* Dermot. That's why you're here. I know all about your little problem from your mother. So, tell me, how many donuts have you eaten today?'

The carpet was suddenly really interesting. 'Dunno. Haven't been keeping count.'

'*Roughly* how many?'

The woman was wearing a white coat just like a real doctor, and her name badge said 'Dr Morlock', but I reckon she just got a certificate off the internet and she was no more a doctor than I was an astronaut.*

For a nutritionist you'd have to say that she didn't look that healthy. You know in those movies where the hero's making his way along a dark tunnel lit only by a spluttering torch, and then a spiked booby trap sort of whips in front of him, with the remains of the last guy who came along the tunnel speared on the end of it? And it's basically just bones but with a few tatty bits of skin attached? Well, that's sort of what she looked like but, you know, *slightly* less dead.

I sighed. 'One or two.'

Dr Morlock's smile changed. It was now the sort of smile you'd turn on a kid who had porridge for brains. I resented that. It wasn't fair. I didn't have porridge for brains. Or for breakfast.

* Just to clarify – I am not an astronaut. I am a twelve-year-old schoolboy.

7

I shrugged. 'Three, maybe.'

Dr Morlock stopped smiling. Now she looked like I'd peed on her chips. Except she probably didn't eat chips. Peed on her lettuce, then. There was anger in her face, as well as disappointment. Her mouth did that cat's bum thing that some mouths do. It's not a good look for a mouth. It's not even a good look for a cat's bum.

It was all too much for me. 'Five.'

The true number was five and a half. I'd bought a box of six. The other half-donut was burning a hole in my trouser pocket.

Dr Morlock shook her head slowly, satisfied at last. 'That really is too many donuts.'

I nodded, but that was just for show. The notion of 'too many donuts' didn't make much sense to me. It would be like saying 'You've got too much money,' or 'You're too good at football.'*

'What I'm going to ask you to do, Dermot, is to write a diary in which you keep a record of all the donuts you eat.'

'A donut diary?'

'Yes, if that's how you'd like to think of it.'

Mmmm . . . that could have been worse. I liked thinking about donuts. It was the next best thing

---

* For the record, I don't have any money and I'm not that great at football.

to eating them. So writing about them wouldn't be *so* bad, would it?

'But not just how many you eat,' continued the mad nutritionist. 'You must also write down your feelings.'

'FEELINGS?!'

Writing about feelings . . . That was *completely* different. Feelings are for the kind of kids who like flower arranging and cute puppies and poetry. Suddenly I was in a whole new world of pain.

'Yes, *feelings*, because it is your *feelings* about your food that are the problem here.'

'Not to me they're not. I like donuts. Is that a crime?'

'It's a crime against good health.'

There was no arguing with Dr Morlock.

'And I've prepared this diet sheet specially for you as well.' She waved a piece of paper at me, like a Jedi with a lightsaber. 'Why don't you ask your mother to step in now, and we'll discuss it together?'

My mum was in the waiting room, reading a yoga magazine. Can you imagine – a magazine about yoga . . . ? It's like having a magazine about verrucas or belly-button fluff. Truly, old people are weird.

When Mum came in, Doc Morlock lost the cat-bum face and went all smiley.

'We'll have a new Dermot in no time at all,' she said. 'You won't recognize him.'

My mum looked quite pleased about that.

DONUT COUNT:

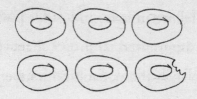

Wednesday 6 September

So this is why I'm writing this diary, wasting precious time in the last few days of the summer holiday. Most definitely *not* my idea of fun.

Everyone knows that diaries are mainly for girls. My sister Ruby had one once. I found it hidden under her mattress, where I was looking for her secret sweet stash. It was full of stuff about her dolls falling in love, and other puke about pop stars she wanted to snog. Or maybe the dolls wanted to snog them, can't remember. It was one of the sickest documents ever produced by the Human Mind. I thought about throwing it in the bin or taking it to school to show my friends, or encasing it in lead and dropping it in a deep ocean to protect mankind, but in the end I decided just to stick a couple of the pages together with a bogey. I remember it was one of those ones that are in the shape of Japan, and are quite crusty at one end but still moist and juicy at the other, and they are always the best ones for sticking stuff together. She never noticed – or at least she never blamed me for it. She probably just thought it was one of her own that had fallen out.*

* I should probably add that now I'm twelve I don't stick stuff together with bogeys any more. Usually. I suppose it's one of those signs of growing up, like suddenly being embarrassed about the jumpers with pictures on them that your parents buy you for Christmas.

Actually, although diaries are mainly for girls, I quite like writing stories. It's the thing I'm famous for at school. When Miss Bean said, 'I'd like you to write a story about . . .' most of the kids would groan and complain, but I used to love it.*

So I suppose I could just look on this as a chance to write stories, except true and not completely made up, like the one I did about getting abducted by aliens who took me to their planet and made me their king and worshipped me as a god, until they realized that I didn't have any special powers and then they tried to kill me, but I defeated them all because human farts were deadly poisonous to them.

Anyway, I spent today hanging out with Jim, my best friend. I've known him since we were

* Well, actually I'd complain and moan too, but just for show.

at nursery together. He's about as normal as a kid could be, except he likes to eat ear wax.

We were sitting on the platform at the top of the climbing frame in the park. We'd kicked a couple of eight-year-olds off, and we had about half an hour before the teenagers came along and kicked us off. That probably carries on until at the end of the day you have a bunch of tough pensioners sitting up there, smoking and drinking alco-pops and jabbering at people passing by.

I'd picked up three donuts from the bakery, one for Jim and two for me, but Jim wasn't hungry so I ate his for him, otherwise it would have been wasted. Everyone knows that you shouldn't waste food because of global warming and the starving children in Africa and all that.

'Sorry you're not coming to Seabrook with us,' said Jim.

'Me too,' I said, although it sounded more like 'mufftuff' because my mouth was full of donut.

Jim was going to Seabrook High, along with nearly everyone else from my junior school. I was going to St Michael's. St Michael's is quite posh, and you're supposed to be brainy to get in. If I'd known I was going to pass the exam then I'd have tried to fail it. It was only because I thought I didn't have a hope in hell that I tried to pass, if you get what I mean.

Mum really wanted me to go there because she's quite snooty, and also she thought there was less chance of me being bullied because of my weight. She didn't understand that the way you avoid being bullied is by being surrounded by your mates, who have all got used to you being a porker.

I think Jim knew that I was a bit worried about the whole thing.

'You'll be all right,' he said. But he wasn't looking me in the eye. Instead he was looking across the park at the houses, even though there was nothing interesting there, apart from a dog having a very long wee. 'But, er, maybe you could think about possibly, sort of, I don't know, getting a bit, you know, thinner.'

Jim had never said anything like that to me before. And suddenly I found that I was telling him about Doc Morlock. I hadn't meant to, because of the massive embarrassment factor, but it just came out.

I thought Jim would join me in making fun of the nasty old cat-bum-mouth, and he did, a bit. But then he said, 'Yeah, but maybe she's right. Maybe you should, you know, eat less donuts.'

I did know, sorta. But I was still a bit annoyed at Jim for saying it. So I said, 'Fewer.' Then he said, 'What?'

'It's *fewer*. If you've got loads of something, you don't say "less", you say "fewer". You'd only say "less" if there was, like, a massive donut, say as big as a tractor tyre. Then you could eat less of it.'

Even as I was saying it I realized that I was being a jerk, and I wished it right back in my mouth. Jim isn't as good at school stuff as me, but he's not an idiot or anything. Because I felt bad I said, 'OK, maybe you've got a point.'

And to show that I meant it, instead of licking all the donut crumbs off from around my mouth and eating them, I wiped them off with my jumper sleeve and then shook them over the edge of the climbing frame, so I wouldn't be tempted to try to suck them up from my jumper later. Anyway, it made Jim laugh, and we were friends again.

DONUT COUNT:

Thursday 7 September

So, yeah, I suppose I've been thinking about my weight. It's not like I'm one of those giant obese kids you get in America, who eat six Big Macs for breakfast and have to be pushed around school in a wheelbarrow. I'm just a normal overweight kid. Every class in every school has a fatty like me. But . . . well, if I could press a button and *not* be fat, then I'd press it. The trouble is that there isn't a button. Being less fat means not eating as many donuts, and that's as hard for me as it would be if you went up to someone else and said, 'Actually, you've been taking too many breaths lately, so from three to four p.m. I'd like you to stop breathing.'

But I'm trying, evil Doc Morlock, I'm trying.

For e.g. I went into the baker's this morning.

'How many today, Dermot?' said Mr Alexis, a friendly smile wrinkling up his face. I was his best customer, so I always got that smile.

I looked at the section of the glass case that held the donuts. Both of the great donut families were represented there. There were the ring donuts, either simply dusted in icing sugar or glazed with different flavoured toppings. Then there were the filled donuts, injected with jam and covered in granulated sugar. If all else failed I'd settle for a filled donut, but my real love was for the classic ring.*

'Just one,' I said. 'Plain, no icing.'

Mr Alexis looked at me like I'd pulled out a gun and demanded all the money in his till.

'ONE?!'

'Yep, one.'

I ate it on the way home. Three bites, savouring each one. Experience had taught me that three bites is the optimum. Eat a donut in two bites and there's a real risk of choking to death. Four or more

---

* The history of the donut is actually very interesting. Archaeologists think they were invented by Stone Age man, who used to cook mammoth bum holes over charcoal fires. Later, Eskimos made donuts out of walrus eye sockets. The modern donut was invented in the 1780s by a French aristocrat, Eduardo D'Nute, who had purchased a large amount of fresh air from a swindler, but turned his misfortune to his advantage when he surrounded small discs of the air with a ring of dough, and sold them at a healthy profit.

bites and I don't get that pleasant feeling of having donut matter touching every bit of the inside of my mouth, with not a single taste bud wasted.

And that's all I've had today. A solitary donut. And everyone knows that a solitary donut – a donut cut off from its friends and companions – is the saddest donut in the world.

In the evening I tried on my school uniform for the first time. My dad's favourite word is 'fiasco', and this was definitely a fiasco.

And I know, by the way, that it was dumb trying on my uniform only a few days before school started, but then that's my family all over.

My mum was too busy to take me shopping with her, so she had got it all off the internet. Nothing was the right size. The shirt I kind of expected. For it to be big enough to fit round my neck meant that the arms hung down almost to the floor. I looked like a shaved orang-utan. The trousers were too tight. Not *way* too tight, which would have been better, because then my mum would have sent them back. No, the trousers were just tight enough to make them uncomfortable, to make me think that undoing the button and allowing my belt alone to keep them up might be a good idea. The blazer – yep, it was *that* kind of school – sort of fitted, but the problem there was that it was PURPLE.

You heard me right, PURPLE.

I'll say it again. PURPLE.

What were they thinking of when they decided to make the blazer purple? I looked like a giant plum.

The new school shoes Mum had got me fitted OK, but they were black and shiny and looked like the kind of loser-shoes the absolute lowest low-down guy in a boring office might wear. The guy who makes the tea for the guy who refills the office stapler. I've seen newly-laid dog poo with more style than those shoes. I'd have been better off tying two biscuit tins to my feet and going off clanking down the road.

NOTE TO SELF: NEVER AGAIN
LET YOUR MUM BUY YOUR
SCHOOL SHOES. OR
ANYTHING THAT YOU
MIGHT HAVE TO WEAR
THAT PEOPLE COULD
POSSIBLY ONE DAY SEE.

Anyway, I came downstairs wearing my uniform and looking like something from the circus. Ruby and Ella were there, along with some of Ruby's pink friends. As soon as I came clumping into the living room in my dog-poo shoes and giant plum blazer, it was as if someone had let off a laughing-gas bomb.* Is anything in life as bad as being laughed at by a gang of teenage girls? No.

My mum frowned and told everyone to be quiet, and said that it wasn't funny and that I looked, er, *lovely*.

Then my dad shouted from the toilet, 'What's going on out there?' which just made the girls

* I don't suppose there's really any such thing as a
laughing-gas bomb, but there definitely should be,
because soldiers can't fight when they're laughing, so
you could easily machine-gun them if you were evil,
or just capture them if you're in a good mood.

laugh even more. Ella didn't say any actual words, but her expression said something like: 'I'm truly embarrassed, in fact ashamed, to be related to you, and I sincerely hope that you've got life insurance, 'cos they're gonna kill you when you get to school.'

Then she went away to hang upside down somewhere in the dark, and the other girls drifted off too, because there's only so long you can laugh at a car crash before it gets boring.

Then I noticed that my mum was crying – not making any noise, just that water-quietly-trickling-out-of-your-eyes crying that sometimes happens when you watch a sad film.

'My little boy's all grown up,' she said in a whispery voice.

Then Dad came out of the loo and said, 'Well, son, you look very smart,' but the impression was ruined a bit by the fact that he was doing up his trousers.

Dinner was something called cannelloni, which turned out to be tubes of pasta nearly as big as toilet rolls stuffed with spinach and covered in a tomatoey sauce. It wasn't actually that bad, although you certainly wouldn't go so far as to call it good. If it was a football team it would have been Aston Villa – you know, not going to win the Premiership, but probably won't get relegated either.

Pudding was a banana.

Hear that sound? The one like a whale singing? That's my stomach rumbling.

DONUT COUNT:

Friday 8 September

As I expect they will feature quite a lot in this diary, I suppose I had better give you the low-down on my family.

I'll start with Mum, who you've already met. Mum's a bit of a Tasmanian devil, in the sense of always being in that crazy spinning motion. But also in the sense of occasionally tearing your head off. She has some kind of a job in some kind of an office where she's in charge of selling some kind of stuff to some other people who then do something with it.

Sorry if that's a bit vague, but it really isn't that interesting, and I've never bothered looking into it much. But she works hard and most of the things in our house are there because she bought them. She's dead thin and has blonde hair, although she has to go to the hairdresser once a month to get it blonderized.

My dad has a more interesting job, although like the Einstein dude said, it's all relative. He does the sort of writing work that proper writers don't want to do. So, he's responsible for the stuff they put on cereal packets, telling you how great you're gonna feel if only you cram enough Krispy Oatballs or Bally Oatkrisps or Oaty Krispballs into your mouth.

His coolest job (remember what I said earlier about relativity?) is writing the descriptions of the aircraft for model aeroplane kits. So, if you really want to know about obscure Italian fighter aircraft of the Second World War, he's your go-to guy.

And right there you've got another problem, meaning where it is you'd have to go to see your go-to guy. The thing is that my dad spends an awful lot of his time in the toilet. In and on. It's kind of his office. He takes his laptop in there and types out his descriptions of Krispy Oatballs or the nimble Fiat G55 fighter. We sometimes see him at breakfast and dinner, but that's about it. In fact, he's been known to eat his meals in the loo as well which, if you ask me, takes the grossness to a whole new level. Hey, I've just had an idea – we should call his laptop his cr— Oh, never mind.

I can't really remember when this all started. He just began to spend longer and longer in there. We hardly even think about it any more. Even my friends, when they come round, know to shout, 'Hi, Mr Milligan,' vaguely at the toilet door.

To complete the pack we have Ruby and Ella, my big sisters. Kind of funny the way 'Ruby and Ella' sounds a lot like 'Rubella', which is like a really nasty disease. And the strange thing is that even though they're annoying in completely different ways they are *exactly* as annoying as each other.

Ruby is all blonde hair and bling. Almost everything she owns is pink, varied only by the odd splash of nice, calming canary yellow.* She has pink things that you wouldn't even dream were ever made in pink. Pink shoes. A pink umbrella. A pink DSi.

I mean, why would you do that to a perfectly decent portable gaming system?

* I'm being sarcastic, in case you hadn't realized.

There should be some kind of organization
to stop that sort of thing. You could call it the
RSPOMTPTSNBMP (the Royal Society for
the Prevention Of Making Things Pink That
Should Never Be Made Pink). And if you're
thinking that all this pink means that Ruby is
nice and fluffy, you'd be wrong. She's as nice
and fluffy as a pit bull. A pit bull with toothache.
A Nazi pit bull with toothache.

If Ruby is a pink attack dog, Ella is what
you'd get if Darth Vader and Countess Dracula
had a baby. Everything about her is black, from
her boots to her hair. Even her lipstick and
nail polish are glossy black. Except her skin,
which of course is as white as a ping-pong ball
because she tries to avoid exposure to daylight,
for obvious reasons, i.e. bursting into flames. She
doesn't say much, not to us anyway, but she hisses

sometimes, like a cat. She spends most of her time hanging out down at the graveyard with the Goths and emos and other Creatures of the Night. It's like she believes that *Twilight* is true, you know, like some TV documentary, and not just a stupid teenage girly fantasy.

Of course, Ruby and Ella don't get on, which is lucky for me because if they're not fighting each other, they're picking on me.

So, yeah, a freaky family.

Anyway, it's tea time now, and my mum is calling me down. And boy, I'm looking forward to it. Friday is fish and chips night. Funny, though – can't smell the usual warm fishy-chippy smell.

In fact I can smell something else . . . vaguely fishy, but somehow not right . . . ?

Saturday 9 September

So, the horror begins.

Here's the story of last night's dinner.

Like I said, Friday is fish and chips night in our house.

Well, it *was*.

So I walked downstairs with that smell – the smell of something that was not fish and chips – getting stronger all the time. Not a rotten smell, but not a nice one either. A smell that could only be described as boiled stuff!!!!

In the kitchen Mum smiled. 'New take on fish and chips,' she said.

It was boiled fish with boiled potatoes and boiled peas.

'Zero fat!' Mum announced proudly.

I thought I was going to cry. 'But it's fish and chips night ...'

'Well, if you weren't such a lard-arse, then we could have proper food,' squeaked Ruby.

'That's enough of that,' said Mum. 'Dermot is on a diet, and we're all helping him by eating the same food. Now dig in, everyone.'

So we started eating. You couldn't say it was disgusting, because it didn't taste of anything. In fact, it was more extreme than that – it sort of sucked flavour out of your mouth. It was anti-food.

Pudding was an apple.

I'd sunk so low that I actually quite enjoyed the apple. Yep, things were *that* bad. Luckily I'd planned ahead and bought a couple of donuts from Mr Alexis. I ate one, and was going to dive into number two, but then I thought better of it and put it back in my underpants drawer, where I kept my darkest secrets and spare donuts.

So, **DONUT COUNT** (for Friday):

Anyway, that was yesterday.

Today is my last Saturday of freedom before I start at big school.

Aaaaaarghhhhhhhhhh!

NOTE TO SELF: ON NO ACCOUNT EVER AGAIN REFER TO SECONDARY SCHOOL AS 'BIG SCHOOL': IT MAKES YOU SOUND LIKE A BABY.

My dad had a talk with me in the afternoon.

'You know your mum only wants what's best for you,' he said.

I shrugged.

'She's got . . . reasons . . . for being like she is. About you and food, I mean.'

I shrugged again.

'All I'm saying is, you know . . . do your best.'

Another shrug. My shrugging muscles were getting quite tired.

'And the truth is, you could do with, you know . . .'

'I know.'

'And I promised your mum I'd help with this,

and not give you treats and stuff.'

Back to the shrugging.

'But I suppose there might be some, ah,
special circumstances or some fiasco when . . .
er, the rules might be allowed to slip. As long as,
basically, you're trying.'

'OK, Dad.'

We had a quick hug and then he went off
again, which was a relief.

Dinner was pasta with tomato sauce. It was all
right, actually.

DONUT COUNT:

Sunday 10 September

The horror continues.

Here's the story.

Sunday is normally the second best food day, after Friday's fish and chips. It's always a roast chicken or something like that. Most days my dad does the cooking because he's always at home while my mum's at work. He's not rubbish at cooking, as long as he sticks to frying things, or doing *exactly* what Mum tells him. But Sunday lunch is Mum's time to cook, and she's good.

Anyway, I came in from spending the morning hanging out at Jim's.

The timing was crucial.

Too early and I'd have to set the table.

Too late and the lunch would be cold, and Mum would give me the Evil Eye.

So I waltzed in, expecting that lovely smell of roast chicken to be filling up the house. Instead there was a different smell. A rotten smell. A smell that could only be described as VEGETABLES!!!!

I went into the kitchen. They were all waiting for me again: Mum, Ruby and Ella, even Dad. Each had a bowl in front of them. It was truly terrifying.

Horrific though the 'food' appeared, it wasn't a patch on the faces round the table. Dad wore the expression of someone who'd reached for

the bog roll, only to find a bare cardboard tube.
Ruby gave me a glare of concentrated pink
hatred. Ella made some kind of mystical sign
with her fingers. It was probably a gypsy curse,
which meant that me and my offspring down to
the tenth generation were going to be blighted
with warts and really bad athlete's foot.

'What's going on?' I asked.

'The new regime,' said Dad, in a voice drained
of all emotion. 'It's really kicked in, big style.'

I stared down at my plate. It looked like a
swamp monster stabbed through the heart with
a carrot.

'Oh,' I said. 'I ate lunch at Jim's.'

'Really? What did you have?'

'What . . . ?' My mind went blank. They were
all staring at me. 'Er, boiled . . .' Boiled what?

'Cheese.'

Cheese! Why on earth did I say cheese?

'Boiled cheese?'

'Yes, er, his family's from Norway. They eat boiled cheese there. It's delicious.'

'Jim's family is from Leeds, as you know very well. Now sit down and eat your *potage de spinach à la carrot* before I lose my temper.'

The rest of the meal passed by in total silence. However, anyone able to read minds would have heard a deafening roar made up of 'I HATE YOU' repeated over and over, coming from the dreaded Rubella.

I tried to put some of the 'food' into my mouth. It tasted as awful as it looked. It was as if I'd followed a camel around with my mouth open.

The one bit of good luck was that my dad got a piece of carrot shrapnel stuck in his throat.

Everyone had a go at whacking him on the
back, which created enough of a distraction for

me to grab a handful of green gunk and cram
it into my sock. After dinner I limped carefully
up to my room, took my sock off, tied a knot
in the top of it and threw it into our next-door
neighbour's garden as a treat for the foxes.

Luckily I had a couple of donuts stashed in
my underpants drawer, so I didn't starve. They
were a bit old and stale, but they sure felt
good in my mouth after all that green filth.
The rest of the day was taken up with me
panicking about the new school, mixed up

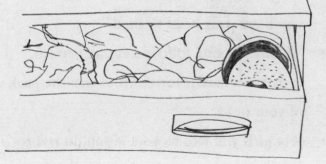

with calmer periods when I just sat in my room quietly dreading it. Ruby and Ella took it in turns to wind me up about what would happen to me. Dad came up later and tried to reassure me, but most of what he said was actually worse than Rubella's wind-ups.

Here's a sample:

- 'Usually, if you really beg them, they'll punch you in the belly and not the face.'
- 'The key is not to let them see you cry. Always cry in the toilets. But never get caught crying in the toilets, because then you'll get your head flushed.'
- 'When you run, follow a zigzag pattern. It makes it harder for them to slap the back of your head.'
- 'No girls will talk to you. If any do talk to you, by mistake or whatever, then just stare

at the ground and mumble.'

- 'At lunch time, don't ever drink anything that is in a jug – it will have been spat in by some kid with whooping cough or consumption.'

I guess this was all based on his experience.

DONUT COUNT:

Monday 11 September

Well, that could have been worse. I might have turned up and the school entrance could have been a portal to one of the Hell dimensions where donuts don't even exist, and I'd have to spend eternity getting stung in the eyeballs by giant scorpions and bitten on the butt by giant tarantulas and totally eaten by giant sabre-toothed tigers although, to be honest, a normal-sized sabre-toothed tiger would have done the job just fine.

My alarm was set for 6.45 a.m.,
which is basically the earliest I've ever had to
get up apart from when we go on holiday and
there's a plane to catch. I was having a nice
dream about— Well, you won't need three
guesses. Except maybe you will, because
donuts don't usually have big white wings
like a swan.

I felt very weird getting dressed in my
clown outfit – I mean, school uniform – in the
morning. I knew that this was a big day. That
I was in a new phase. That things had changed
for ever. Mum chatted to me while I ate my
Weetabix (I had three) but I couldn't really
hear her because of all the thoughts in
my head.

I had to get the bus to St Michael's. My
mum would have driven me but there was

no way I was letting her kiss me in public view
on the first day. I wasn't *that* dumb. I pretended
that I preferred to take public transport because
of global warming and saving the rainforest.
My dad came with me on the bus. It was a big
wrench for him to leave his toilet, so I suppose
I should be grateful.

He did a triple flush before he emerged.

Outside the school, Dad patted my shoulder
and wished me luck. We both knew that
anything like a hug would be very bad news
for my credibility. The weird thing was that I
actually wanted a hug. But a pat on the shoulder
it was, and then Dad headed back towards the
safe refuge of our toilet. I was on my own.

I followed the steady stream of kids through
the gates. There were three tall boys and a tall
girl standing there. They had badges on. I peered

to see what one said. Then the guy whose badge I was peering at grabbed the back of my head and rammed my face against the badge.

'Prefect,' came a voice that was both a sneer and a shout. 'You blind as well as fat?'

A slightly more friendly voice said: 'Newbie, Ivan, give him a break.'

'Sure, leg or arm?'

They all laughed, including the tall girl, and I scuttled past.

The schoolyard was mental. There were millions of kids of all shapes and sizes. Most of the kids were already in little clumps and gangs. I felt the loneliest I've ever felt in my life. I saw one other boy standing on his own. He had black hair that flopped carelessly across his face. The hair made it hard to read his expression, but I thought that maybe he also looked a bit

lonely, so I decided to go and say hello. I walked

towards him and opened my mouth, pleased at

having thought of something to do, rather than

just standing around like a dummy.

'Get lost, fatty.'

He'd said it before I'd even uttered a sound.
His lips hardly moved when he spoke, as if it
wasn't worth the effort. I realized that the look
on his face wasn't loneliness. It was withering
contempt.

NOTE TO SELF: NEVER AGAIN GO UP TO SOME KID YOU
DON'T KNOW AND TRY TO MAKE FRIENDS.

I wandered away, bumping into more kids,
and others bumped into me.

The school building was in two parts. One
was made out of red brick and looked about a
thousand years old. The other part was glass and
concrete. The old part appeared solid enough
to last another thousand years, but the new part

looked like it was about to fall down.

I reached into my blazer pocket and found my donut. I'd meant to save it till break time, but this was a crisis. My standard three bites and it was history.

Then a klaxon blared. It sounded like a five-minute nuclear warning and made me want to hide. Suddenly kids were forming up into lines, patrolled by teachers and more of the prefects. After some shoving and jostling and shouting, the lines marched off towards the school building. It was a bit like a military parade, but performed by the worst army you ever saw, worse than the Italians or, I don't know, the Paraguayans or something. You wouldn't want them guarding your borders. You wouldn't really want them guarding your sock drawer.

After a while I worked out that it was just Year Sevens left, but it still seemed like a big crowd. I guess there were about a hundred and fifty kids.

Then a small baldy man in glasses raised a megaphone to his lips.

'*ARSHPLAJZBUTUNICORD*,' he said, or something like that – it was hard to tell because the megaphone distorted his voice so badly. More mangled shouts from the megaphone. Shoving, elbowing. Other teachers and prefects moved among us. The message got through. We were being put into classes.

'*DURSHNUTMILLINSHA.*'

It took a couple of seconds to de-scramble it in my head. Dermot Milligan, i.e. *me*.

The baldy man pointed towards a line. This was it, my form class.

I was relieved to see that the floppy-haired kid wasn't there. The line moved. We went into the school. There was a strong smell of cabbage and sweaty feet, which was pretty impressive as there can't have been any cabbage or sweaty feet in the place for months. I imagined for a second that this was where cabbage and sweaty feet came to get their smell. It made me smile. There was a girl looking in my direction. I think she thought that I was smiling at her, and she tutted and tossed her head.

I blushed.

Bad start.

Then we were in a classroom. I found a desk in the second row, right on the edge next to the window.

The teacher was introducing himself.

'Hi, I'm Mr Wells,' he said, his smooth young

face shining in the morning light. He seemed quite nice. 'I'm your form teacher, and I'm sure we're all going to be good friends.'

Someone sniggered behind me.

'Well, that's me, now I'd like to find out who you are,' continued Mr Wells. 'I'd like you to stand up, one at a time, and tell me your name and, let me see . . . yes, what your favourite thing is.'

There was a big collective groan from the class – the first thing we'd all managed to do together.

'Well, let's start with you,' said the teacher, pointing to the girl sitting in front of me.

It seemed that Mr Wells began almost every sentence with the word 'well', which was kind of ironic, given his name. I wondered if they were connected.

There was an expectant pause. The girl stood up slowly. I realized it was the same girl who'd thought I was grinning at her earlier. She had raven-black hair. She'd obviously been in the shop when her parents bought her uniform, because it actually seemed to fit her.

'My name's Tamara Bello,' she said in a slow voice.

I don't mean to sound like a softy, but it was kind of . . . I don't know, *nice,* you know, for a voice. It made me think of donuts dunked in hot chocolate.

'And I like pulling the wings off flies.'

There was a shocked silence, then a kind of nervous giggle from the class.

'Well, that's great, Tamara,' said Mr Wells.

Most of the other kids kept it straight after that. Pretty boring, really. You know, 'My name's Robert and I like to play on my computer' sort of thing.

My turn was coming round, and I thought I'd try to play it for laughs. I could mention that I liked donuts, and maybe give my tummy a bit of a pat. It was a high-risk strategy, but I thought it was worth it. It might just get the class on my side. I'd learned that if you can make fun of yourself before the other guys do, then it takes away the sting.

Then Mr Wells was smiling at me. I stood up too fast and my stomach caught the front of my desk and knocked it flying forward, right into the back of Tamara Bello's chair. Everyone laughed like crazy, and even Mr Wells had a bit of a smile, though he tried to hide it.

Any normal person would have spun round to see what was going on, but Tamara turned

slowly, like an owl, and gave me a look of . . .
well, I'm not sure there's even a *word* for it. Her
skin was like milky coffee, and I felt funny inside,
like I'd eaten one donut too many.

So now I was in a double fluster. I picked up
the desk, but somehow managed to knock over
my chair. I was blushing again and my hands

were as sweaty as two boil-in-the-bag kippers.

Finally I got everything picked up. I cleared my throat and announced loudly, 'My name is Donut, and I like Dermots.'

That was it. I was doomed.

'Donut! Donut!' they all chanted.

In a vision I saw what was going to happen.

My name was no longer Dermot. My name was Donut and there was nothing I could do about it.

For the next couple of hours the kids in my class got what fun they could out of calling me Donut. Actually, most of it was fairly harmless, except for some horrible little kid who said, 'Knock knock.'

I sighed, and said, 'Who's there?'

'Donut.'

'Donut who?'

'Donut ask me again or I'll punch you.'

Then he punched me on the arm, quite hard. Some kids laughed, even though it was as far away from funny as Earth is from Alpha Centauri.*

The best thing about today was that we got

* That's a star 4.37 light years away, in case you didn't know.

sent home early, just before lunch, which was
supposed to make it a nice gentle introduction
for us.

I got some chips and ate them on the
bus on the way home. Then I ate my second
emergency donut, which was supposed to
be used only if the first one went missing in
action.

Of course, Dad wanted to hear all about
it when I got in, as did Mum when she got
home later from her office.

'What were the teachers like?'

'Did you make any friends?'

That sort of thing.

I answered with nods and grunts, which
didn't really satisfy anyone.

For dinner we had risotto, which means
rice with bits in it. I don't really know what

the bits were. Might have been courgettes in there. The truth is, it might have been stuffed pterodactyl and I wouldn't much have cared.

DONUT COUNT:

Tuesday 12 September

I knew it was going to happen. At morning break today I went out into the yard and a load of kids yelled out, 'Here comes Donut.'

Then another group shouted, 'He likes Dermots!'

It wasn't just the kids from my class, so word must have leaked out.

I saw the floppy-haired kid. He didn't join in with the chanting, but there was something about the way the other kids glanced over at him, as if looking for his approval, that made me think that he was behind it.

I just went and found a quiet corner and waited, with my head bowed, for break to be over.

Fat and alone.

After break we had geography, with Mr Braintree. His beard blended into his tweed jacket, so you couldn't tell where one ended and the other began, which was quite interesting. More interesting, at any rate, than finding out that the biggest export of Ecuador is bananas.

Then it was lunch time. I walked by myself to the dining hall, which was in the ancient part of the school. The smell should have warned me what was coming, but I figured that nothing could possibly taste as bad as that smell smelled, which was maybe kind of naive. I joined a queue and picked up this sort of tray thing with different compartments. It was exactly like being in a prison movie, and I kept looking over my shoulder to make sure nobody was sneaking up to stab me in the back with a shank made from a sharpened toothbrush.

I shuffled along in the line for a while until I reached the serving counter. Then a dinner lady, working like a sort of decrepit robot, put a big dollop of mashed potato on the tray with one hand and a piece of grey rubber on top of the potato with the other. We were supposed to help ourselves to a mixture of peas and carrots. I put one pea and one piece of carrot on my tray. Then another dinner lady spooned out what can only be described as frogspawn and added a spoon of red gunk in the middle of it.

'Excuse me,' I said, 'what's that stuff?'

'Jam.' The dinner lady didn't seem to have
any teeth.

'No, I mean the other stuff.'

'Tapioca.'

I was going to ask her what tapioca was, but

I was shoved forward
from behind. Anyway,
I knew what it was.

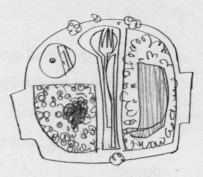

It was poison.

So, there I was with
my prison tray full of poisonous slop. I looked
around the big hall. There were kids everywhere.
Talking, shouting, laughing, screaming. One kid
was even eating. Most of the tables were already
full. I saw one empty chair and walked towards
it. When I got near, I realized to my horror that
the floppy-haired kid was there. Actually, writing
out 'floppy-haired kid' all the time is taking too
long, so from now on I'll call him the FHK.

One of the other kids – one of those pale
kids who don't seem to have any eyebrows or
eyelashes – looked at me and said, 'Get lost, fat
boy. This table is for Xaviers only.'

The FHK leaned over and whispered
something in his ear. The pale kid laughed
and the rest of the table joined in.

'Only kidding,' said the pale kid. 'Sit right
down.'

I didn't want to. I *really* didn't want to. But I
couldn't think of what else to do, and then there
was always the faint chance that these kids might
be OK after all. So I sat down, gave a weak little
smile and got ready to make some conversation.
I think I might have been on the verge of talking
about the weather, or last night's telly. But before
I could even open my mouth the seven kids
(the tables sat eight) all got up. One by one they
came round and emptied all their disgusting
food on my tray, so it piled up and spilled over. It
looked like a dinosaur had taken a dump on the
tray. Then they all took their now-empty trays

and raced out, giggling like girls. Except for the FHK, who had the same blank face as usual.

I was stunned by all this. I knew they'd played some kind of trick on me. Kids on other tables started to point and laugh as well. Then I felt a tap on my shoulder. I turned and looked into the face of Tamara Bello.

'You understand what's happening here?' she said in that voice of hers like melted chocolate.

I shook my head.

'Anyone who doesn't finish their lunch gets a dinner-hall detention.' She pointed towards the exit, where a teacher was checking the dirty trays that the kids were piling up.

'A what?'

'You'll find out.'

'But, but . . . they can't! It's not fair!'

'Life isn't fair. Tuck in.'

Then Tamara Bello was gone.

I stared at the mound of muck on my tray. Of course, I couldn't eat it. It looked like *it* might be able to eat *me*. I thought about trying to explain what had happened to the teacher on guard. But I couldn't say who had done it, partly because I didn't know the names of the scumbags, and partly because even if I had known I couldn't have said, because if you squeal on people, that's it, you're finished – you may as well just go and flush your own head down the toilet.

So I was stuck.

Then something clattered down in front of me. It was an empty tray. I looked up into a funny little face I recognized from my form class. Little, that is, except for the front teeth, which were as big as shovels. All things considered he couldn't have looked more like a rodent if he

was playing the part of King
Rat in the panto.

'I picked up two trays by
mistake. Just leave that mess there
and show the empty tray to the
teacher. Do it quickly before
anyone notices.'

He had a funny way of
talking – every so often he'd
make a sort of '*ungth*' noise. So it
sounded more like – '*Ungth* I picked up two *ungth*
trays by mistake. Just leave that mess there and
ungth show the empty tray to the *ungth* teacher.'

'OK, thanks,' I said, still in a bit of a daze.

'*Ungth* like, er, *now.*'

A gang of kids were leaving and I joined in
with them. I dumped the empty tray and I was
out of there!

And I think I'd made a sort of friend.

I ate three plain donuts on the way home. I
reckoned this was OK, as I'd definitely got
my average down. Before I went to see Doc
Morlock I was on four a day. Since then I'd been
averaging about two. So I could have three and
still be heading in the right direction.

DONUT COUNT:

Wednesday 13 September

Things a bit better today, in the sense that
nothing really terrible happened. I hung out
with my new friend, the goofy short kid. Turns
out he's called Renfrew, which is one of those
names that you sort of half think might be funny,
but you're not sure why or how. I've decided to
forget that he looks like some kind of vole or
whatever, and also to ignore the fact that he goes
'*ungth*' all the time, as he's the only friend I've
made, so far. Anyway, he's probably writing in

his own diary right now about how his only friend is a tub of lard called Donut, who happens to like Dermots.

Anyway, Renfrew came up to me after morning registration and said: '*Ungth* that was pretty pants what those Xavier kids did to you yesterday.'

I agreed that it was, indeed, pretty pants, and I thanked him for helping me out. And that was it, we were friends. Then Renfrew told me all about the thinking behind who gets put in what form, which had been baffling me. He's got a brother in Year Ten, so he understands it all. This is how it is.

The ultra-brainiacs are all in Campion. I'm quite glad I'm not in Campion because they get extra homework. The next brainiest, who also seem to be the coolest, get put into Xavier.

Xavier is definitely the form to be in, not least because it begins with the undeniably cool letter 'X'. And guess who's in Xavier? Yep, the FHK. Actually, I don't have to call him the FHK any more because Renfrew told me he's called Steerforth. But guess what? I'm going to carry on calling him the FHK, because this is my diary and I can do what I want in it.

The sporty kids are all in Newman. They all look like the Incredible Hulk, except for being green. I mean, *not* being green.*

And then there's us, Burton. We get everyone who's not outstandingly brainy, not very cool, and not very good at sport. We have plenty of nerds, though.

* I suppose, if you looked like the Incredible Hulk and were also green, then you would, in fact, *be* the Incredible Hulk.

Or, as Renfrew put it: 'Basically, we're Hufflepuff.'

Dinner tonight was baked potatoes with low-fat cottage cheese. It was edible, in the sense that your own snot is edible if there's nothing better to do with it.

I told Mum and Dad about my new friend, and that cheered them up. Dad agreed that Renfrew was actually a funny name, but he didn't know why either, although he thought it might have something to do with Count Dracula. My dad knows all kinds of stuff, not all of it useless.

Had a bit of a relapse later with the donuts. The trouble is that Mr Alexis is having a 'Donuts of the World' promotion at the bakery.

There were donuts there that *might never be seen again*!!!!

So I sampled:

- the Canadian maple syrup
- the Belgian chocolate
- the Chinese cherry blossom
- and the Bavarian sausage flavour.

Good eating, one and all!

DONUT COUNT:

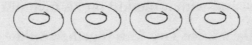

Thursday 14 September

Well, that was unexpected: made another new
friend today. It's official: I now have a gang!
I think it was because of having Renfrew to
hang around with. One kid on his own just
looks like a loser. Two kids together, on the
other hand, look like a party about to happen,
even if they are a couple of drongoloids like
me and Renfrew and the party is likely to be
one of the worst in the history of partying.

The first kid to be drawn into our gang

was basically a lamppost doing an impression of a human being. His name is Simon Palmer and he's not only the tallest kid in the year, but practically the tallest in the school. Tallest and skinniest, so I don't think he'd be much use in a fight, unless you used him as a sort of a lance.

And because he's miles taller than anyone else, you spend all your time looking right up his nose, and he's got these really complicated nostrils, with all kinds of funny flaps and lumps that you don't expect.

Everyone calls him Spam. Spam talks in this really, really deep voice, like Treebeard off *The Lord of the Rings*.

'You sound like Treebeard off *The Lord of the Rings*,' I said, and after a few seconds he laughed, which is when I knew we'd be friends. I had to explain the joke to Renfrew because he hadn't

read the book or seen the film, which is
pretty freaky. Although he usually sounds
like Treebeard, Spam's voice sometimes goes
all high and squeaky, like a chipmunk. It's
quite funny when that happens.

Together, me, Renfrew and Spam look like an illustration in a textbook, showing the different types of human boy: the fat one, the midget, the beanpole.

DONUT COUNT:

Friday 15 September

Now there's a fourth member of our gang.
I thought that we already had most of the weird
bases covered, but it turns out there was one
missing: the square base. This kid, you see, is
made out of squares. Or, more accurately, cubes.
His head is a cube. His body is a cube. Even the
different bits of his legs are made out of cubes.
He looks exactly like one of those pictures of a
robot they used to draw in the olden days, before
they thought of fluid metal cyborgs and robots

with realistic skin and hair and stuff.

Normally, looking like a really out-of-date robot would be the weirdest thing about a person, but with this kid it was only the *second* weirdest.

'Corky's got a problem,' said Renfrew.

We were sitting in the dining hall. In front of us were trays piled with misery, the name of which was toad-in-the-hole. Toad-in-the-hole is supposed to be made from sausages (the 'toad') and Yorkshire pudding batter (the 'hole'). But this one seemed to have been made out of real

toads and the hole part was the hole at the back
of a rhino, through which it slopped out
its claggy poo.

'We've all got a problem,' I said, jabbing at a
toad with my fork. It hopped out of the way.

'He's got something called Tourette's
syndrome,' Renfrew continued.

'I've heard,' said Spam in his low-down voice,
'of that,' he added with a squeak.

'I haven't,' I said. 'What is it?'

'It's when you can't stop yourself from
blurting out bad words and other things you
shouldn't say . . .' Renfrew explained.

'Yeah, I can see that that *is* a problem.'

'No, you don't get it. He also has a really bad
stammer.'

It didn't properly sink in until Corky started
to speak. Well, *speak* maybe isn't the right word.

His square face went purple. He opened and closed his eyes. His ears began to wiggle. But all that came out of his mouth was:

'*F-f-f-f-f-f-f-f-f-f-f-f-f-f.*'

Then a pause, followed by:

'*K-k-k-k-k-k-k-k-k-k-k-k-k-k.*'

I looked at Renfrew.

'Philip Cork,' he said. 'It's his name.'

'Oh,' I said.

It was kind of fascinating to watch, in a car-crash kind of way. Which was probably why half the kids in the dining hall were staring at us. The 'us' included four other nerds. They weren't nerds like us, i.e. blatantly obvious, screaming, flagrant nerds. They were more the quiet, semi-invisible kind of nerds that nobody really notices or cares about. A couple of them already had zits, which you'd have thought would have had the decency to wait until puberty came along. It was so unfair – like having rotten teeth even though you never ate any sweets. Some of them *had* rotten teeth too, crossed over or gappy or green. And they all had seriously terrible haircuts, as if a flock of mutant birds had come down and nested on their heads.

I felt kind of embarrassed to be on the same table as these guys, but I also felt grateful that I had some people to sit with. I looked around. The FHK was on a table with his cronies. I also saw Tamara Bello sitting with a gang of girls. And she saw me. She looked at me, then looked at the other freaks on my table, then shook her head. If we were flies she'd definitely have pulled our wings off by now. I couldn't quite decide who I hated most, her or the FHK.

Actually, I've just realized. That's it – I've survived my first week at St Michael's. The worst is over.

The worst *has* to be over. Celebrated with three donuts, although I am determined to keep it down to two or less from now on.

DONUT COUNT:

Saturday 16 September

Funny, this whole keeping a diary thing. I'm not saying I *like* it, but I actually don't hate it as much as I thought I would. Kind of gives me a way to get my head in order. It makes me think about things. Some of these things aren't very nice to think about, but that doesn't mean that you don't have to do it. Like brushing your teeth, I suppose. I mean, no one really *likes* brushing their teeth, do they? But you do it because you don't want to have green teeth.

And one of the things it made me think about is being fat. Like I said, being a bit porky at junior school was OK. I had Jim and my other mates. They took the mickey a bit, but only the way you do with your friends. But now it was different. I'm in a new place with new friends. And new enemies. So maybe it's not just the fear of Camp Fatso that makes me want to cut down on the donuts.

I called Jim on his mobile (I haven't got one as Mum says they give you brain cancer, and anyway you're not allowed to have them at St Michael's). He sounded a bit down, which sort of cheered me up. He's coming over tomorrow.

I think Mum and Dad knew it had been a hard week, and everyone was vaguely nice to me today. Even Ruby and Ella. Well, not *that* nice. They just ignored me, but not in the usual

'I hate you' ignoring way. Just ordinary ignoring, without any hate in it.

For dinner, Mum cooked loads of nice things. It was even arranged as a starter, main course and dessert, just like in a posh restaurant. We had smoked salmon for the starter, which I quite like even though someone once told me it's not even the remotest bit cooked, but completely RAW. And then we had grilled chicken, despite it not being a Sunday. And for pudding we had something called sorbet, which is like an ice lolly without a stick, and which didn't totally suck.

DONUT COUNT:

Sunday 17 September

Jim and me were lounging around in my room, surrounded by loads of junk. My mum had told me that unless I tidied up a bit she was going to come in with five bin bags and throw everything out. But tidying your room is famously the hardest job in the world, except maybe being the Queen's Official Bum Wiper (my dad told me she has a special person to do it for her, and she's really fussy about it being done properly, and he says if you don't do it well enough that counts as treason, which still has the death penalty.)*

'So are things OK at Seabrook then?' I said to Jim.

He put his finger in his ear and had a good old root around. 'It's all right.'

'Pete and Ben and The Other Jim are there too, aren't they?'

I should say here that there was another Jim at my junior school. He was quite boring, so everyone called him The Other Jim. I reckon even his mum called him The Other Jim.

'Yeah,' said Jim – not The Other Jim, but my Jim, the real Jim. 'But it's different now. They've got new friends and . . .'

He just trailed off. I didn't know what to say.

* I don't actually believe in the Queen's Official Bum
  Wiper any more, by the way, although I did when
  Dad first told me about the job.

94

Then Jim cheered up by himself. He looked around.

'Your mum's right. There's a lot of junk in here, isn't there?' he said.

'Not really. It's just my stuff.'

'Nah, most of this is embarrassing. It's gonna have to go.'

Now *I* looked around, and began to see things for the first time. Yep, he was right. There were things here that could destroy me. Plus, frankly, there was hardly any room to sit. So we divided everything into three piles:

KEEP

CHUCK

DUNNO

The KEEP pile was heavily electronics-based, and basically represented the past two birthdays and Christmases, plus some money my granny gave me before she went ga-ga (I wasn't allowed to keep the money she gave me *after* she went ga-ga). It had all my PS3 games, my DSi (not pink, but a nice, decent white), my iPod, that sort of thing. They weren't going anywhere, although I did have a sneaking suspicion that the DSi didn't really cut it any more.

The CHUCK pile was on the small side, because I kept taking things out of it that Jim put in. The biggest item was some kind of toy animal. Couldn't tell you exactly what kind. Maybe an aardvark. Possibly a sloth.★

Anyway, this *thing*, the toy *whatever,* was pretty beat up. It had been part of the family

★ Don't get me wrong – I'm good on animals. In the wild, I'd be able to tell a sloth from an aardvark. Sloth: upside-down in a tree. Aardvark: er, well, actually I don't know much about aardvarks.

for a long time, and it showed. Ruby and Ella
had really put it through the wringer. Ruby
had cuddled it to within an inch of its life and
then finished it off with a yellow ribbon noose
around its neck. Then she'd daubed pink nail
varnish on the corpse. Ella had shaved off its
fur and put staples all over its poor floppy ears
and gouged out its eyes, probably to use in
some kind of voodoo ritual.

The girls had called it various names (Sweet Pinky Boo Boo, Kushaaar Vulture Lord of Thraaall, etc. etc.), but I didn't bother with the whole naming business, because I couldn't bear to get too emotionally attached to what was clearly a profoundly damaged individual.

As well as the animal, there were a couple of Lego bricks so tightly jammed together you'd need dynamite to blow them apart, so they weren't much use for anything other than throwing at Ruby and Ella, and I had better tools for *that* job.

The DUNNO pile was a lot bigger. It had things in it that I knew I wouldn't ever use again, such as swords, bows, shields, toy cars, Junior Scrabble, Junior Monopoly . . . all that kind of stuff. But the thing is that even though I knew I wouldn't be using them again, they all had good memories. It also had all my *Star Wars* Lego, loads of Warhammer, some rare action figures – the evil black Spiderman, for e.g., plus the whole set of *The Lord of the Rings* figures, including the very rare and hard-to-come-by Witch King.

'Remember,' I said to Jim, 'when we swapped round Ruby's Barbies and Ella's demon puppets, and they united their forces and came for us and we had to fight them off, and I was wearing my Roman Centurion outfit—'

'And I had this crossbow.' Jim pulled the trigger on the crossbow, despite the fact that the arrows had been lost at least three years earlier, and even the string was nothing but a memory.

Jim looked at the Lego and other stuff in the DUNNO pile. '*Star Wars* is a bit lame . . .'

he said. 'Remember that Jedi lunch box I had last term?'

'Yeah.'

'I deliberately lost it so my mum had to buy me a different one.'

'What did you get?'

'Just plain. Totally er, *unthemed*. No icon, no logo, no nothing. It's the only way to go. Anything else and you know you're going to regret it in three months' time.'

I nodded.

I was impressed with Jim. His thinking had progressed lately, and he was obviously now at a higher stage of development than me.

'It's sometimes useful,' he said, 'to have a big brother to kneel on your chest and slap your face and tell you exactly what it is that's lame about you.'

'I've got sisters to do that.'

'Sisters just aren't the same. They can tell you you're a rubbish dancer, and let you know that you've got uncool hair, but the important stuff, you know, which toilet cubicle to hide in when there's a maths test, how to spit on the back of a dorky kid's head in the dinner queue without them realizing it, how to give a decent dead leg . . . for all that, you need a guy's touch.'

'Yeah,' I agreed.

The fact that girls couldn't give a decent dead leg was one of those basic truths about the universe that only a lunatic would deny.

'Look,' said Jim. 'Deep down you know what we have to do . . .'

I nodded.

Five minutes later we were standing around the

big pile of leaves in our back garden that Dad had been heaping up ready for burning for as long as anyone could remember.

We looked at each other. Jim said, 'It's for your own good.'

'I know.'

And then on went the Lego, the Warhammer, the weird mutant cuddly animal – in fact everything from the CHUCK and DUNNO piles. I'd got the special giant matches from the kitchen (the ones I wasn't supposed to touch) and used one to light the pile.

I was burning my childhood. It was an authentic Rite of Passage, like when Maori boys get their first tattoo, or Eskimos snog their first walrus.

I felt my eyes begin to water. At first I thought it was because of all the emotion.

It's not every day you say goodbye to your childhood.

Then I realized it was because of all the black oily smoke coming off the burning plastic.

We moved back. It was quite impressive. There weren't any decent flames, but there was a red glow from underneath the tangled pile of old toys, and so much smoke you'd have thought a battleship had been torpedoed and dive-bombed to destruction.

It was about then that I heard the first faint siren. And by siren, I don't mean a beautiful sea maiden trying to lure me onto the rocks - I mean the electronic wail of a police car.

Or, as it turned out, fire engine.

'What the hell's going on?'

That was my dad, leaning out of the upstairs toilet window.

'We're just—'

But I never

got any further, because then a

bunch of fire-fighters wearing

breathing apparatus and carrying

axes crashed through the fence

from next door. Behind them I caught sight of

Mrs Baxter, our nosy neighbour, who must have

called the fire guys, which was a pretty
sneaky trick.

And then my mum came out, her face as hard
as the stuff they put on the nose-cone of the
space shuttle to stop it burning up on re-entry,
and my sisters were right behind her, followed
by my dad, fastening his trousers.

I got banned from *everything* for a week.

DONUT COUNT:

NO
donuts

Monday 18 September

Maybe I should have guessed what was coming.
Looking back now, I reckon that maybe there
was a funny feeling in the air. But, well, I've
had a lot on my plate (most of it inedible), so
I maybe wasn't at my sharpest.

Anyway, I strolled through the school gates
this morning, not realizing that I was about to
have the worst three minutes of my life.

I saw Spam, Renfrew and Corky standing
over on the far side of the schoolyard and

I began to walk towards them.

After a few steps I heard a hideous sort of . . .
I don't know, *honk*.

I turned round and saw that loads of kids
had formed a line a few metres behind me.
Probably just twenty or so of them, but it
seemed like more somehow. All boys. Some
of the kids were grinning, but most of them
were trying to look normal. Except that no one
normal ever looks the way people look when
they're trying to look normal, if you get what
I mean – you know, whistling and looking up
into the air as if something really interesting
is happening up there, a skydiver or mid-air
explosion.

I felt that wave of panic you feel when
you're on your own up against something
really bad. Panic mixed up with embarrassment.

And futile rage. My only thought was to get to the safety of my friends. I turned back round and walked on a bit more quickly.

The honking came again. Each pace brought another huge, rumbling honk, exactly in time to my steps.

Honk

Honk

Honk

I spun round. There was a flurry of action, but I couldn't make out what was going on. The kids were all from my year. A couple from my class, but mainly kids from Campion and Xavier. I recognized some from the FHK's gang, including the pale kid with no eyebrows.

I walked on again.

Honk

Honk

Honk

Honk

Again I turned to face them. This time I managed to catch sight of someone disappearing behind the others. He'd obviously come to the front and then been shunted back again into hiding as I turned.

And I saw something else – a gleam of golden metal.

I started to blush. And sweat. I noticed that my shirt had come out at the front and I wanted to tuck it in, because it looked so stupid, but I didn't want to stop. They were all grinning now, but still trying to hide it.

One person caught my eye. Slightly apart from the others: the FHK. *He* wasn't grinning or trying not to laugh. He was just staring at me, his face as blank as a painted wall.

I walked away more quickly, just short of a run.

Honk

Honk

Honk

Honk

Honk

I started to run.

Honkhonkhonkhonkhonkhonk

Now it really did seem as if the whole school was laughing at me, not just the kids in my year. Even the prefects, who should have been helping me, were laughing. An older kid tried to trip me up, for no reason at all – just, I suppose, to join in with the others.

You think this all sounds bad? Believe me, it was about to get much, much worse. Remember what I said about my trousers being too tight, and so sometimes I'd leave the top button undone?

You probably guessed back then what was going to happen, didn't you?

Well, it happened now.

Yep, my blinking pants fell down.

Down. Fell. Pants.

Down all the way to the ground, like something you'd see in a stupid old film from the days of black and white and no sound. I started to pull them up, but realized that meant pointing my backside at the crowd, and that felt wrong. So I pulled them up as I spun round for the last time.

They were all now laughing so much that they didn't bother to hide what they were doing. I saw what the kid who'd been lurking at the back was carrying. Actually, he wasn't carrying it, he was *wearing* it. It was this massive brass instrument, coiled around him like a fat golden python. I don't even know what they call it – a tuba maybe, or a euphonium.

. . . Well, I've just gone and looked it up on the internet. It was one of these:

A sousaphone, it's called. Named after a bloke
called . . . Oh, I can't be bothered.*

They must have got it from the music room –

* Sousa. Or Phone. Or Sousaphone. Probably not
  Sousaphone, because then the instrument would
  be a Sousaphonaphone.

they had all kinds of stuff up there.

Anyway, this kid was blowing away on it tunelessly, except he now couldn't blow because he was laughing so much. Suddenly the whole gang of them lost control, and they laughed like it was some kind of laughing competition with a million pounds going to the winner.

And the thing is that I sort of got the joke. Fat kid walking, tuba, *honk honk honk,* trousers fall down, yeah, funny. It was so funny I was about to cry.

As well as the FHK, I saw Tamara Bello standing with a group of girls. She wasn't part of the gang that was following me, and she wasn't laughing. In fact, her face was just as blank as the FHK's had been. But somehow it was a different sort of blankness and I just didn't know what it meant.

That moment there, facing the pack, was the loneliest of my life. And then suddenly I felt that there was someone at my shoulder.

'Come on, Donut,' said Renfrew, making his usual *ungth* noise, as if he was swallowing each word.

Spam loomed up on the other side. 'Jerks,' he said in his Treebeard voice.

'B-b-b-b-b-b-b-h-h-h-h-h-h,' said Corky.

Together we turned our backs on the crowd and walked to registration.

The rest of the day was a bit of a blur, though I don't think anything else really bad happened.

When I got back that afternoon I went straight up to my bedroom. My dad knocked on the door and came in and looked at me for a while and then went out again. Half an hour later he came back with a bacon sandwich and a donut.

He's OK, my dad, sometimes.

DONUT COUNT:

Tuesday 19 September

I gave it the works this morning. I began with gruesome gut-rot (food poisoning), moved on to shivers and aches (malaria), foaming at the mouth (rabies), before finally throwing myself on the floor and lying completely still without breathing (death).

Nothing doing.

'Forget it,' said Mum. 'You're going to school.'

It turned out not to be that bad. I was pretty nervous when I came in through the gates, and

people did stare and nudge each other, but
as for being followed around by a gang of
brass-instrument wielding bullies, zilch.

After registration which, to be honest, I don't
remember much about, Tamara Bello came up
to me. She stood there with that haughty look
on her face and said something. I was expecting
it to be nasty and clever at the same time – the
sort of insult that only sinks in
after a few minutes.

'I thought it stank,'
she said.

'What?'

'Stinky and stupid. And
not even funny.'

I still didn't know quite
what she was on about.

My pants falling down?

Stinky?

'Eh?'

'That stuff with the tuba yesterday.'

'Sousaphone,' I said, and wished immediately that I hadn't.

'What?'

'It was a sousaphone, not a tuba. A tuba is . . . a . . . different . . . shape . . .' I trailed off. Tamara had already turned away before I'd finished speaking. Fair enough, really.

Dinner tonight was a joy. My mum went out with her work friends. She left strict instructions about what we were supposed to eat. I give no more detail than that it involved rocket and walnuts. Whoever gave the exciting name 'rocket' to what is basically lettuce should be put in jail, or possibly just plain executed and offered – as their last meal – a plateful of the vile green stuff. The thing about rocket is that it gets rid of the one acceptable feature of lettuce, i.e. it tastes of nothing, and replaces it with a definitely bad thing, i.e. it tastes of the last bit of running sick you chuck up after all the chunks have already made their appearance.

But no rocket was to be eaten tonight. Not by me, at least. Dad ordered pizza.

I had a double-meat feast. It included bits of almost every animal ever domesticated by man, including llama and water buffalo (and possibly, though I don't want to dwell on it, dog).

Afterwards, I lay back and burped my first contented, satisfied burp in days. Underneath the usual fungusy burp smell, there was a definite hint of roast llama. Ruby ran out of the kitchen

waving her hand in front of her face, and Ella
did some dry retching, but that just meant that
I got to eat the rest of their pizzas too, which I
did even though they were both having plain old

margaritas. People who like margarita pizza are like people who like ready-salted crisps – they just don't know how to enjoy life.

Dad cunningly put the pizza boxes in next door's recycling bin so Mum wouldn't find out about what he'd done.

All finished off with a couple of donuts. Suddenly life is OK again.

DONUT COUNT:

Wednesday 20 September

Everything in life has to be paid for, and today I paid for the fact that yesterday didn't stink. By which I mean that today stank worse than my now famous llama-flavoured burp of last night.

Anyway, nothing terrible happened until the fourth period, which was English. The English teacher is called Miss Brotherton. She's all elbows and knees and has a long bony nose and generally looks a lot like a woodpecker.

After we'd sat down, she said that we had

to name our favourite book. Tamara Bello said hers was the *Collected Short Stories* of Anton Chekhov, who she said was some Russian writer who was better known for his plays. I didn't believe that for a second. I don't mean about him being better known for his plays, I mean that his rubbish-sounding stories was Tamara's favourite book. It's probably the *Hello! Magazine Christmas Annual.*

When it was his turn, Renfrew said that his favourite book was *The Lord of the Rings.* My gob just fell open. He gave me a sort of 'Hey, I'm sorry, but what could I do?' look.

Miss Brotherton was really impressed. 'An excellent choice, William,' she said.

Of course, it was exactly the book I was going to choose, but now I couldn't say it without looking like a complete suck-up/loser.

It threw me into a mad panic, and I couldn't think of a *single* other book I've *ever* read, even though I've read, like, *millions*.

Miss Brotherton was staring down her enormously long nose at me and the sweat was bursting out all over my face. And then Tamara Bello gave me another one of her looks-without-a-name, but this one got across pretty well the idea that I was a dimwit who had never read a book in his life. I half remembered some titles. Half remembered the names of some of the authors. I opened my mouth, thinking if I did that the name would pop out.

Well, something did pop out.

'THE BIBLE.'

That got an even bigger laugh than 'My name's Donut', although not quite as big as the sousaphone fiasco.

'Well,' said Tamara, in her slowest, most chocolatey voice, 'that at least explains the shoes.'

So now everyone thinks I'm one of those kids who reads the Bible in bed and probably has 'Jesus Loves Me' written all over his pyjamas. Even Miss Brotherton looked a bit embarrassed for me.

I don't know, I seem to have some kind of a social death wish. First there was the 'My name's Donut and I love Dermots' incident, then the Bible thing. You'd think that it would be enough for fate to make me fat without also making me a massive doofus.

Ate two donuts in my room. One South African go-go berry flavour and one Peruvian guinea-pig flavour. Just kidding about the guinea pig. Mr Alexis gave me a plain old jam

and I was happy for the length of time it was
in my mouth.

That's enough diary for one day.

DONUT COUNT:

Thursday 21 September

Came in this morning and there, waiting for me, was the same gang of kids who'd ambushed me with the sousaphone. They all knelt across the path and put their hands together and started praying loudly. I pushed past them but they got up and followed me, shouting 'Alleluia', 'Praise the Lord', and that sort of thing.

Quite funny, I suppose. For some reason it didn't get to me the way the sousaphone incident did. But I still really wished that the

earth would open up and swallow me. Actually,
no, I hoped the earth would open up and swallow
them down into its core of molten
iron and burn them to a crisp.

In the afternoon it was PE. Except it wasn't,
unless PE stands for 'Particularly Embarrassing'.
Our PE teacher is called Mr Fricker. Mr Fricker
has no hands. The word was that he lost them in
a terrible accident involving, depending on who
tells you:

- a helicopter
- a lawnmower
- the Taliban
- an angry dolphin
- a sausage-making machine
- one of those rotary pencil sharpeners
  with a handle you have to turn round
  that went wildly out of control

However it was that he lost his hands, whether torn off by polar bear or gnawed away by ants or dissolved in acid, nobody would ever make fun of Mr Fricker. This wasn't just because it's wicked to make fun of people who have lost their hands (or anything really, except maybe unimportant things like a toe or their bus pass). No, you wouldn't make fun of Mr Fricker because he's the most terrifying human being who ever lived.

He has two ways of talking. One is very quiet and sinister. It's the kind of voice a serial killer would use to lure you into his basement.

The second way of talking isn't talking at all but SHOUTING INCREDIBLY LOUDLY.

The shouting incredibly loudly began in the changing rooms. My PE kit was as tight as a piece of cling film wrapped round a block of cheese, and it took me longer than anyone else to get changed. So Mr Fricker stood about six centimetres away and screamed:

'MILLIGAN, NOT ONLY ARE YOU TOO FAT BUT YOU ARE ALSO AS SLOW AS A SLOTH IN TREACLE! GET YOURSELF CHANGED, BOY, BEFORE I GO AND FETCH A ROUNDERS BAT AND USE YOUR FAT HEAD AS A BALL.'

The word 'ball' was so loud, a bit of plaster actually fell off the ceiling, as if we were in a bunker under heavy artillery fire.

Of course, all the other kids were sniggering because it wasn't them being screamed at, but then Mr Fricker glared round at them too, the changing-room lights glinting off his baldy head.

After that we just sat in rows while Mr Fricker gave us a long speech about personal

hygiene. The boys, that is – the girls were at
the other end of the gym getting a similar talk,
I imagine, from Miss Gunasekara, Mr Fricker's
second-in-command. At the end of our talk,
Mr Fricker glared at us all for a bit longer,
then he said:

'I suppose some of you are thinking that
because of my . . . *hand issue*' – at this point
he raised his handless arms – 'I'm not able to
compete at the highest sporting level. But I
assure you that I can still beat any one of you
at any sport you care to mention.'

Then he went into his private office, which
is a corner of the gym with a curtain around it.
Renfrew was sitting next to me. 'He's a complete
nutter,' he whispered in my ear. Then, as if to
illustrate the point, Fricker sprang out. We were
all amazed. At the end of one arm, fastened using

some elaborate metal attachment, was a ping-pong bat. On the other side he had a hockey stick, looking a bit like a stretched pirate's hook. I don't mean the pirate had been stretched . . . Oh, you know what I mean.

'He's a cyborg,' I said to Renfrew, quietly.

But not quietly enough.

Fricker's ears swivelled to pick up the sound, then he zoomed over, his legs a blur.

'WHAT DID YOU SAY?'

'Nothing, sir,' I said, trembling.

'Nothing. Nothing. Nothing. Nothing. Nothing,' said Mr Fricker in his scary quiet voice.

Then he blew.

'ARE YOU CALLING ME A LIAR?'

It echoed round the gym, and the girls at the other end all looked up.

'N–no, sir.'

'THEN TELL ME WHAT YOU SAID!'

My mouth opened up, but nothing came out.
I was terrified. I thought Mr Fricker was going
to ping-pong my head.

'He called me a sideboard.' That was Renfrew
speaking.

'What?' said Fricker, looking like he'd just
found a small piece of dried poo in his bag
of crisps.

'It's my nickname, sir.'

Fricker stared from me to Renfrew and
back again. You could tell that he wanted to
hook someone round the neck with his
hockey-attachment, and then maybe hoist
them into the air and send them flying across
the gym, but he couldn't think of a good
enough reason.

'Never talk again in my class,' he said in the end to both of us. 'Or you'll wish you'd never been born,' he added, but you knew his heart wasn't in it.

DONUT COUNT:

(Scandinavian loganberry, Swiss cheese, and Scotch haggis. Thank heavens it's the last day of the Donuts of the World promotion.)

Friday 22 September

Not even going to mention school today.
Which isn't because it was so awful that I don't
want to think about it (it was actually one of
those inbetweeny days when nothing either
great or rubbish happens). No, it's because
after school I had my second visit to Satan's
nutritionist, the gruesome Doc Morlock.

We were standing in front of her wall. There
was a chart on it. On my bedroom wall I have
a chart of Second World War fighter aircraft.

This was a very different type of chart.

It was a poo chart.

It looked like this:

BRISTOL STOOL CHART

Type 1		Separate hard lumps, like nuts (hard to pass)
Type 2		Sausage-shaped but lumpy
Type 3		Like a sausage but with cracks on its surface
Type 4		Like a sausage or snake, smooth and soft
Type 5		Soft blobs with clear-cut edges (passed easily)
Type 6		Fluffy pieces with ragged edges, a mushy stool
Type 7		Watery, no solid pieces Entirely liquid

Doc Morlock had a stick. She pointed at the little round poos on the chart – Type 1.

'This is what we want to avoid at all costs.'

She pointed to Type 2.

'This is hardly any better. Sooner or later these will kill you.'

I nodded, imagining myself being chased around by little hard poos wielding Samurai swords. I don't mean to imply that little hard poos are at all Japanesey, because that would be racist – just that whenever I imagine myself being chased by anyone or anything, they usually have a Samurai sword. It's one of my quirks.

'What I want to see,' Doc Morlock continued, 'is a Type Three or Type Four. A nice long smooth stool, pointed at both ends, with a texture like warm fudge. That indicates a proper, healthy diet, full of fibre. It's the stool of champions. Now, Dermot, take the stick and point to your stool type.'

I took the stick. I imagined how nice it would be to shove it right up Doc Morlock's nose and into her brain. I was blushing so much my face had gone beyond red and into the purple zone. I couldn't look at her horrible, disgusting chart. Couldn't bring myself to point at any of her horrible, disgusting stools.

'Don't know, I never look.'

'Well, from now on you must, Dermot. You must. By the way, did you bring the diary with you?'

'Diary? Er, no. I didn't know I was supposed to ...' I thought about all the stuff I'd written in the diary. Secret stuff. *This* stuff.

'Well, you were. How else am I to monitor your progress? Now, strip down to your pants and we'll take those measurements.'

DONUT COUNT:

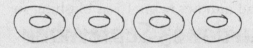

Can you blame me?

Saturday 23 September

My mum had to go into work today, even though it's the weekend, so Dad took us swimming. I'm actually pretty good – I can beat Ruby and Ella at the crawl. But that's probably because vampires like Ella are water-soluble, and Ruby spends all her time checking out the boys and convincing herself that they are checking her out right back.

As Ella was swimming along, her hair dye and mascara and stuff dissolved, leaving a long black stain in the water.

Ruby was wearing a pink swimming costume
that you could see from space. The best part
was when she was doing sidestroke so she could
look at this muscly kid on the high board, and
so she didn't notice a manky plaster that was
floating in the water and she sucked it into her

mouth and choked on it and then ran into the
changing rooms going '*Aaaarrrrrggggghhhhhh*
aaaarrrrrggggghhhhhh aaaarrrrrggggghhhhhh!!!!!!!!!!!!'
with everyone staring at her and thinking she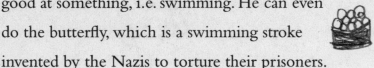
was a nutcase, which was brilliant, really.

  Dad's not a bad swimmer either, which you
wouldn't really expect from a guy who spends
most of his time in the toilet. Or maybe that's
exactly what you should expect? When he gets
in the water he changes from my not-much-use-
at-anything dad to a different dad – a dad who's
good at something, i.e. swimming. He can even
do the butterfly, which is a swimming stroke
invented by the Nazis to torture their prisoners.

    Afterwards, I was famished – like you always
are after swimming. I gave Dad one of my
pleading donut looks, but he said we were going
to try something new.

The new thing turned out to be sushi. Yeah,

that's right, raw — and I mean
totally raw — fish, wrapped up in
cold rice. Yum yum. (That's a sarcastic

yum yum, by the way.) What kind of madman
invented that? We all complained about it, but
Dad insisted we at least try it. It probably
helped that they were having a half-price
promotion at the sushi bar. My dad finds it hard
to buy anything that isn't on special offer.

So we sat there not hoping for much and a
nice Japanese lady came and brought us green
tea that tasted of nothing at all (which I'd

count as a result, as green tea sounds like
it ought to taste of hot snot). And then

the sushi came. It looked quite OK, so
I tried a bit. Then I tried a bit more. Dad told
me to eat it with some of the slivers of ginger

and a tiny bit of some stuff that looked like green toothpaste but which turned out to be the hottest, spiciest substance ever invented, and is probably radioactive. But when it's all in your mouth, it tastes amazing.

For pudding we had these weird little Japanese donuts with sesame seeds on top. Not a real donut, but better than no donut at all.

Not a bad day at all, really.

DONUT COUNT:

(if we're counting the sushi donuts)

Sunday 24 September

Another nice day. With one exception. Me and Jim went and chucked stones in the canal. That might not seem very interesting to you, but sitting with your back against the wall lobbing stones into the water and hearing the lovely round 'plop' is surprisingly satisfying, especially when it isn't peeing down with rain.

I told Jim about some of the rubbish things that were happening at St Michael's, but I said it in a way that turned it into a joke, and that made me feel a bit better about it all.

He told me that things weren't that great at Seabrook High, which also helped to cheer me up, because hearing about other people's troubles is always nice. Apparently there was some psycho kid called Garry Martin who'd decided he hated Jim and was going to batter him after school one day. But Jim said his big brother, Chaz, was going to give Garry Martin a 'Chaz Special'. This involved Chaz kneeling on your chest and dribbling drool down onto your face. He thought that would discourage Garry Martin from bothering him, and I tended to agree – it would discourage me from doing pretty well anything, including breathing.

Then Jim asked, 'What are your new mates like, then?'

'Oh, they're OK. Quite cool, really,' I replied,

throwing another stone in the canal so I didn't have to look him in the eye. Everyone knows it's OK to fib to your mates as long as you don't look them in the eye when you do it. Otherwise, if they find out, they tell everyone that you lied to them and did it while you stared right into their eyes. Yep, definitely way worse than ordinary lying.

And just then who should I spy coming along the canal towpath but Renfrew. Not looking cool *at all*. He was walking his slightly jerky walk and you could see his lips moving as he talked to himself, which was one of his weird little habits. I didn't think he'd seen me.

I know what I should have done. I should have waited till he reached me and Jim and introduced them and let Renfrew hang out with us for a while, chucking stones into the canal and talking about our favourite flavours of milkshakes.

But instead I got up and said, 'Let's go to the shopping centre,' and then I just walked away and up the stone stairs that take you from the canal to the road.

I felt really bad about what I'd done, although I wasn't sure exactly why. It wasn't like I'd bullied Renfrew or thrown him in the canal or made fun of him, was it?

Hang on.

I suppose that if there's any point at all to a diary like this it's to have a poke around in your own head to try to understand what's going on in there. I did know why I'd avoided Renfrew. It was because I was ashamed of him. There. It's out. He was about the least cool-looking kid in the universe, and I was worried that Jim would think that I was uncool too.

Writing that made me feel a bit sick. Truly, the

human soul can be a dark and dismal place.

Sunday lunch was OK – salmon baked in tin-foil parcels, with potato wedges and broccoli. I found that if you just eat the fluffy bit at the end of each sprig it doesn't really taste too much of actual broccoli, although you still get that faint feeling you've walked into a room five minutes after someone has farted.

I had a sneaky couple of donuts up in my room. I thought they might make me feel better about running away from Renfrew. But it worked the other way round – thinking about Renfrew ruined the donuts. It felt like trying to swallow lumps of cement.

DONUT COUNT:

Monday 25 September

As I've got to think of something I can put in my donut diary that I could actually let Doc Morlock see, I thought I'd try to describe some of the teachers. I haven't really mentioned them much, except for Psycho Fricker, Woodpecker Brotherton, Hairy Braintree and nice Mr Wells.

For maths we have Mr Kennilworth, who looks like a poodle surprised in the act of licking its own bottom. He's OK. He knows a lot about maths, but doesn't know anything about how to control the class, so people just talk all the way through his lessons.

Mr Khan teaches chemistry. He's pretty funny and tries to tell at least one joke per lesson. When I say 'pretty funny' I mean by teacher standards. By normal human standards, he isn't that funny.

Here's a typical Khan joke:

'Why do all the other subatomic particles hate the electrons?'

'I don't know.'

'Because they are so negative!'★

★ Just in case you don't know, electrons have a negative electric charge, whilst protons have a positive charge and neutrons a neutral charge. Blimey, I can be boring, sometimes.

Yeah, well, I warned you.

Mr Beal teaches RE. His main job seems to be to show you how unhappy believing in God can make you.

The Head of the Year is called Mr Whale – he was the short bald man with the megaphone on the first day. You get sent to him if you do something really bad. He then breathes his eggy breath all over your face as a punishment. Or so I've been told – I haven't been sent to him yet.

The headteacher is called Mr Steele. He only ever appears for Friday assembly. He mumbles a few words, then shuffles back to his office. He wears carpet slippers and has fantastically hairy ears, which tells you all you really need to know about him.

Dinner at home was spinach risotto. No comfort there. Dad ate his in the loo. I think he may well have cut out the middleman and flushed it straight down the pan.

Today was one of those rare days when one donut seemed like enough. Not quite sure why. There is something incomprehensible deep down in the soul of every person, I suppose.

DONUT COUNT:

Tuesday 26 September

Rained like a dog today, so we had to stay in our form rooms at break.

I did some more work on the made-up Donut Diary to show to Doc Morlock. Renfrew and Spam helped me out.

I put in the bit about there being something incomprehensible in the soul of every human being, which I thought made me sound pretty deep. The best bit was this, though:

'I gazed out of my window and saw a tiny

little bird pecking at the hard ground. It looked like it was probably starving. In fact it was definitely soon going to be lying on its back with its legs in the air, totally dead. I was going to eat a small donut, but the little bird looked at me with such sad eyes that I crumbled it up and threw it out of the window. The bird gobbled up the donut crumbs and then flew away without even whistling a quick thank you, which I thought was pretty rude. But I didn't mind because I knew I'd done the Right Thing and saved its life by sacrificing my donut. But then, that's the kind of person I am.'

It was Renfrew's idea to put 'gazed' instead of plain old 'looked', as it's more poetic and thoughtful.

While we were working on the diary,

Corky showed off his epic farting ability.
He doesn't have to wait for one to come along,
but just does them when he wants to. So, if
you say, 'Corky, give us a fart,' he just does.
Amazing, really.

It didn't amuse Tamara Bello much, though.
She'd been reading her book of Chekhov
short stories, but when the smell reached her
she used the book to waft the smell back, then
threw it at me, as if I'd been the one who was
farting. Turns out Chekhov packs quite a punch
when it gets you in the middle of the forehead.

I kept meaning to talk to Renfrew about

my disappearing act on the canal but the chance
never came up. He probably didn't notice it . . .

DONUT COUNT:

(Mr Alexis's donut counter was completely
empty. He gave me a stale muffin out of
sheer pity.)

Wednesday 27 September

At morning break today the FHK came up
to me.

'We haven't properly met, have we?' he said.

I'd only ever really heard him say, 'Get
lost, fatty' before. His voice was so posh he
sounded like someone off the telly. I don't mean
EastEnders, I mean posh telly – the news or
something. He stuck his hand out and continued,
'My name's Paul Steerforth.'

I didn't know what to do. This was my enemy,

my tormentor, and now he was being friendly. Almost by itself my hand went out to his, and he shook it firmly.

'I'm—' I was going to say Dermot, that being my name, but for some reason I stopped myself. 'I'm Donut,' I said defiantly.

The FHK smiled. He had very white teeth. 'Good to meet you, Donut. I just wanted to say that I'm sorry about the other morning. I tried to stop those kids . . . that stupid prank with the tuba—'

'Sousaphone,' I said.

'What? OK, whatever. Anyway, I thought it was pretty poor behaviour. I believe in giving everyone a chance. That's all, really. See you around.'

Then he clapped me on the back and wandered off. I asked Renfrew to check my back to make sure he hadn't stuck on a 'kick me' sign, but it was clean.

All very mysterious.

Soup tonight for dinner. Leek and potato. It would have been OK if it hadn't had the leeks and potatoes in it. Makes you sort of wonder what the stuff is in leek and potato soup that isn't leek or potato. Is it just soup? Reminds me of a sort of joke I heard once (one of those jokes that aren't really very funny, but still manage to stick in your head).

Q. *What's the white stuff in bird poo?*
A. *Well, that's bird poo too, stupid.*

Anyway, I ate three bowlfuls and still felt hungry, because everyone knows you can't get full on soup. Ruby and Ella ended the meal by fighting about whether *Twilight* was rubbish because it was too gloomy (Ruby) or not gloomy enough (Ella).

I sneaked off and had a cinnamon donut, which is my least favourite kind of donut, but the only one Mr Alexis had left. The fact that it was the last one makes you wonder why they bother making them, as obviously nobody really likes them. Is it because there's some law about using up all the cinnamon so it doesn't cover the world like volcanic ash and kill us all? Or maybe the guy in overall control of world donut production likes cinnamon donuts and is forcing his warped tastes on the rest of us. I suppose we'll never know.

DONUT COUNT:

Thursday 28 September

FHK was friendly again today. He didn't say anything to me, but he waved and smiled when he was with a group of kids, and I found myself waving back.

'Maybe he's not so bad,' I said to the guys.

Renfrew went '*Ungth.*' Corky said, 'B-b-b-b-b-b-b-h-h-h-h-h-h-h,' and then he did a short, sharp fart. Not sure what it meant. Might just have been clearing his throat, if you see what I mean. Spam didn't say anything.

What's weird is that I've now gone three whole days without being humiliated. What gives?

But today's main event wasn't the FHK's weird friendliness. It was my next encounter with Doc Morlock, the worst so far.

'Good afternoon, Dermot,' she said.

Already her mouth was pursed and her nose wrinkled as if I'd brought a bad smell into the consulting room with me. Actually, I'd done a little tummy squeak before I came in, so I probably had.

'Hi.'

'And how is the new regime coming along?'

'The new . . . ?'

'Your diet and exercise plan, Dermot.'

'Ah, yeah, not bad.'

I studied the ceiling. It wasn't very interesting, even by ceiling standards (which are low), but it was better than looking into that face with its cat-bum mouth and cruel eyes.

'You have the journal?'

I nodded, reached into my school bag and passed her the fake Donut Diary. I'd drawn some donuts on the front cover. Then I'd drawn some dinosaurs (a triceratops, a T-Rex and a brontosaurus, to be precise) eating the donuts. And then I'd drawn some fighter planes attacking the dinosaurs. The fighter planes were a combination of Spitfires and Hurricanes with some modern jets of my own design, plus the Red Baron's Fokker triplane, which was probably the coolest plane in the history of aerial warfare, even if it hovered on the edge of being really silly. Just one more wing – if it had been a Fokker *quatro*plane — and it would have been a laughing stock. There's an important lesson in there somewhere, although I'm not sure what it is . . .

I'd drawn the fighters because I was a bit worried that kids of my age shouldn't be interested in dinosaurs any more — it's only one step up from having a special blanky and getting a goodnight kiss from your mum. Anyway, they were some of my best drawings, although I hadn't got the neck on the bront—

'Dermot!' snapped Doc Morlock.

'Yes?'

'Am I seriously supposed to believe this?'

'Well, er, yes, I guess so . . .'

'Let me read this back to you. "Fourteenth September. Went for a quick half-marathon after school. Snacked on three brazil nuts and a handful of raisins. Dinner was broccoli quiche with steamed broccoli on the side and chilled broccoli mousse for pudding."'

The secret to a good lie is that you mingle up some truth with it. We really did have all that broccoli muck. The broccoli mousse was about the most disgusting thing I've ever eaten. I made a joke about it being broccoli that had been pooped out of a moose (you know, an animal like a big, gormless deer).

'You can ask my mum,' I said, putting on my good little angel face.

Doc Morlock stared at me. Then she said, 'Let's see, shall we? Just step on the scales.'

I did. On tiptoes, which makes you a little bit lighter.

Sixty-one kilograms.

The first time it had been 61.5.

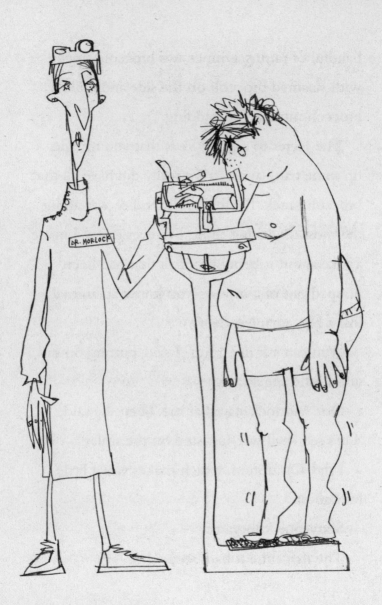

I was actually quite pleased with that. My cutting down from four donuts a day was having some effect.

But Doc Morlock was not impressed. 'This won't do,' she said, shaking her scrawny head. 'Won't do at all.'

'It could be that some of my fat has turned into muscle . . .' I sort of trailed off as Morlock did her cat-bum mouth thing, then I added hopefully, 'I've heard that muscle is, er, heavier than fat.'

She looked at me in the same way a vulture would look at a dead wildebeest.

'Do you have a secret desire to go to Camp Fatso?' she asked, her voice eerily soft.

I looked down – I couldn't meet that cold, inhuman eye – and I shook my head.

'All I'm asking for is for a little honesty. At the

moment we're living a lie, aren't we, Dermot?'

She was too strong for me. I nodded.

'What will it be like, Dermot?'

'Pardon?'

'Your stool.'

'I don't know.' I was still looking down. I was in hell, I really was.

'Show me on the chart, Dermot.'

I stood up and moved over to the wall. I looked around for Doc Morlock's special pointing stick but I couldn't see it.

'Just use your finger, Dermot.'

Slowly I pointed to the Type 3 stool, the one that was labelled: *like a sausage or snake, smooth and soft*.

'That's what I'd *like* to see, Dermot. But if what I see is this' – she leaped up and was suddenly right beside me, pointing at Type 1 –

'if what I see is nasty little hard balls, then you know where you're going, don't you?'

'Camp Fatso,' I murmured.

Then what she had said sank in. 'See . . . ?'

'Yes, *see*,' she snapped and I recoiled, as if from a slap. 'I need a stool sample.'

'Stool . . . ?' Against all logic I still vaguely hoped that she might be referring to the thing you sit on.

'Number twos,' she said, rapping the chart with her knuckles. 'One of these. I need to analyse exactly what you've been eating, and that's the only way to get at the truth.'

I felt suddenly very dizzy. And panicky. I actually sort of hoped I might faint, which would get me out of this INCREDIBLY EMBARRASSING SITUATION. But I stayed annoyingly conscious.

'B–but I don't think I could go now. I mean,
I went this morning and . . .'

'Not *now*, Dermot. When you next come
in – I want to see you again in about two weeks.
Use this.' Doc Morlock rummaged in her desk
and handed me a clear plastic bag, containing a
small plastic tub.

I don't really know what happened in the rest
of the session. The next thing I know is that I
was staggering out of there. I probably burned
my way straight through the wall using my
red–hot face.

DONUT COUNT:

I know, I know. But what do you expect? From tomorrow I cut down. I have to.

Feelings? Work it out for yourself.

Friday 29 September

Really don't know what to do about filling the little pot that Doc Morlock gave me. There are two problems. Number two problems, you'd call them if you were trying to be funny.

The first was: how on earth were you supposed to get *it* into the pot? You'd have to have the aim of Robin Hood, plus the ability to stop at exactly the right moment, or else ... Well, I'll leave that up to your imagination. There were other ways, but they were even more disgusting.

And if you're imagining those, then I suggest you stop, right now. I did wonder if maybe they'd given me the wrong sort of container. One for little people. With little poos. What I needed was something bigger . . .

Then there was the even trickier problem of the poo itself. Doc Morlock was going to do her scientific test on it and find out exactly what I'd been eating. Then she was going to feed back to my mum.

Then it was Camp Fatso. Plus I'd feel like I'd let everyone down, which is even worse. OK, feeling like you've let everyone down isn't, actually, worse than being sent to fat prison, but it's still pretty rubbish.

But what could I do? I couldn't talk about it with the guys at school. Somehow news would spill out, like poo from Doc Morlock's little pot.

Couldn't even talk about it with Jim. It was just too embarrassing and yucky.

Stop eating donuts, then?

Unthinkable.

Even thinking about thinking about it is unthinkable, which is why I'm not going to think about thinking about thinking about it.

All this not thinking about things is making me hungry. And what do I have in my secret drawer?

Ah yes, two fresh, moist, succulent, irresistible donuts.

DONUT COUNT:

Saturday 30 September

Renfrew came round today, along with Corky. It was a bit weird having a play date with my new mates.

NOTE TO SELF: IT'S NOT A PLAY DATE WHEN YOU'RE AT BIG SCHOOL. IT'S JUST CALLED 'HANGING OUT'.

NOTE TO SELF: HOW MANY TIMES DO I HAVE TO TELL YOU ABOUT USING THE TERM 'BIG SCHOOL'?!!!!!

Corky seemed a bit more relaxed than he
was at school. His stutter was still really bad,
though, and it took him about ten minutes
to say hello. Renfrew sort of looks after him,
which is kind of nice.

We were in my room when Corky did
this fart that sounded exactly like that song,
'Yes, We Have No Bananas'. It was about the
funniest thing I've ever heard. Also pretty gross,
of course, especially when you considered that
I had to sleep in that room, and the fart gas
was going to linger in there for some time,
hanging under the ceiling or lurking behind
the curtains.

Actually, it didn't smell that bad, considering
how long it had gone on for. Jim says that
short farts are more pungent, but I've always
thought it was the really long ones that do

the damage. My theory is that the first bit
of the fart is fairly harmless as it's really just
froth and air. But once you get down to
the last dying bit of a long fart, you've got
some really toxic stuff in there. It's the dregs,
and there's more to it than just gas. We're
talking chunks. I know the fairly innocent
Corky long fart seems to weigh in on Jim's
side of the question, but that's because we're
ignoring another dimension – the loudness.
As everyone knows, the silenter a fart is, the
more deadly. So you have to integrate that
fact with the data we have about the duration.

You need to think about it like a graph.
If the duration of the fart represents the
x-axis, then the loudness of the fart is the
y-axis, with the loudest fart at the bottom
of the axis.

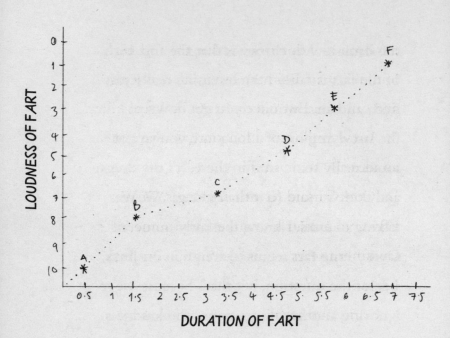

For any fart, the toxicity (i.e. poisonousness) is measured by plotting both the length and the loudness of the fart. The worst farts are the long, slow silent ones. The least nasty are the short loud ones.

In the example here (all these farts are hypothetical), Fart A is the least noxious, as it has both low duration (or length) and high loudness. Fart F, on the other hand, is long and quiet and would therefore be a real killer.

Anyway, all this stuff about farts gave me an idea.

'Corky,' I said. 'If you can sing "Yes, We Have No Bananas", couldn't you sometimes say other things, you know, using your butt? I mean, when you get stuck.'

Corky thought for a moment, looking deadly serious. Then he lifted up one buttock and farted a clear and distinct 'Yes!'

We laughed so much that my dad came out of the toilet to see what was going on.

A bit later Jim came round, but I asked my dad to tell him that I wasn't in. I wasn't ready yet to mix up home and school friends. My dad gave me a funny look and began to say that it was wrong to tell lies for no good reason, but then went and did it anyway.

I think he understood.

DONUT COUNT:

Sunday 1 October

I had to do a family tree, for history homework.
We were supposed to stick in pictures of any
relatives we could find in the right place in
the tree diagram. We have a load of family
photograph albums in the cupboard under
the bookshelves and I got them out and had a
look through. All the usual baby pictures: plenty
of embarrassing ones of me on the potty, etc.,
plenty of pink ones of Ruby, and lots with Ella
staring moodily into the camera, like she's got

terrible deep dark thoughts, even though she's only three.

There were other albums with pictures before we were even born. Pictures of Mum and Dad looking happy. These days my dad looks depressed and my mum looks cross or busy, but in these pictures they were always smiling or laughing. And sometimes, disgusting though it is, snogging. I mean, why would you start *snogging* when someone's about to take your picture? It's just plain crazy. Snog some other time. Or, better still, DON'T SNOG AT ALL.

Then there were even older albums with pictures of my dad when he was a kid with Uncle Kevin and Granny and Grandad. And there was an album with Grandma and Grandpa, Mum's parents, that is. But, weirdly, there were hardly any of Mum in them. There were some of when she was a baby, and then a toddler with yellow hair and blue eyes, but none of her as an older kid, a teenager or whatever.

Anyway, I knew that I couldn't just rip the photos out of the album, so I banged on the toilet door and asked my dad if there were any loose pictures I could use. He huffed and puffed and then went up into the loft and came down with a carrier bag full of photos.

'Have a look through this lot,' he said, and disappeared back to the loo.

I poured the photos out onto the living-room floor. Most of them were just rubbishy versions of the ones in the albums, with someone looking the wrong way or their mouth at a funny angle or everything out of focus, except for a pigeon flying past. And then I saw something truly weird. There was a picture of a fat girl. It looked a bit like Ruby, except it was obviously from the Olden Days because of the clothes.

Then the door opened and my mum came in.

'What's all this mess?' she shrieked. And then her face went hard and white, like stone. And suddenly I realized who the fat girl was.

It was her.

My mum.

My super-yogarized, incredibly skinny mum.

She came over and shoved all the photos back in the carrier bag, without saying a word.

So, that's it. That's why she's so bothered about me being a bit overweight. She'd been a fatty.

At least it took my mind off the poo.

Until now.

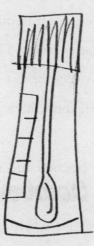

The little pot is on my windowsill. I can hear
it calling me in its mocking voice.

'Fill me. Fill me. If you dare.'

DONUT COUNT:

NO
donuts

Monday 2 October

The general weirdness continues. Today it was Tamara Bello, of all people. I was putting some stuff in my locker, and when I closed the door she was there. I think I might have let out a little squeak.

NOTE TO SELF: DO LESS SQUEAKING.

Tamara, as usual, looked at me like I was something she'd squeezed out of a spot. Not that she's got any spots. Her skin is so perfect you'd think she was a cyborg. She probably *is* a cyborg. One of the ones that gets sent back from the future. I don't know yet if she was sent back to destroy me or to save me. Maybe she was just sent back to ignore me, although I suppose that would be pretty stupid, and they probably just shouldn't have bothered.

'You should watch out,' she said.

'Eh?'

NOTE TO SELF: DON'T SAY 'EH?' WHILST WEARING A GORMLESS EXPRESSION: YOU LOOK AND SOUND LIKE A *VILLAGE IDIOT.*

'Steerforth.'

'Eh?'

DID YOU NOT LISTEN TO THE LAST 'NOTE TO SELF'? WHAT'S THE POINT IN WRITING THESE THINGS DOWN IF YOU DON'T PAY ATTENTION!

Then I remembered who Steerforth was.

'Oh, the FHK.'

Now it was Tamara's turn to look puzzled, although she didn't say 'Eh?' or look particularly gormless.

'I mean the Floppy-Haired Kid.'

A tiny little twinkle appeared in her eye. 'Yeah, him.'

'Sorry, what was it about him?'

A huge tut from Tamara. 'I don't know why I bother.'

Then she was gone.

DONUT COUNT:

Tuesday 3 October

Right, so as well as all the small footie games
that go on around the yard, there's this massive
football match that begins on Monday and
ends on Friday and basically anyone can join
in. Well, in theory. Obviously me and my mates
aren't the world's greatest footballers. Renfrew
and Spam basically can't play at all. AT ALL. I
don't just mean that they're rubbish, I mean that
Renfrew can't kick the ball without falling over,
and Spam never even manages to make contact

with the ball but just swishes away like someone practising a golf shot with their leg.

Corky isn't that bad, but he loses his temper and randomly runs around kicking anything that gets in his way – kids, walls, the ground, whatever, so no one ever wants to be on his team. I'm basically OK at football – not good, but not totally useless either, but I'd never got up the courage to play in the Big Match because of all the chances to get snubbed and humiliated.

Actually, the humiliation would start at the picking. The way they do it is for the two best players to 'step it out', which means that they stand facing each other like two gunslingers, and then walk towards each other, and the one whose foot goes over the top of the other's gets to have first pick. Then they take it in turns until everyone's used up.

I knew what would happen if I tried to play. The group of the unpicked would get smaller and smaller until at last it was just me, like the last manky mutant donut left on Mr Alexis's shelf. (I usually get that one anyway.)

And three guesses who is always one of the captains? Who else but the FHK? The other was usually a big bruiser called Jonathan Body.

The FHK was pretty skilful. He was one of those players who doesn't need to run around much. He'd just look up, play a little dummy, leaving some other kid on his backside, and then slide exactly the right pass to some other kid who was doing all the running around for him.

But then today I was vaguely looking at the captains as they were picking, sort of half thinking that it might be quite nice to play, and the FHK shouted out, 'I'll have Donut.'

I was totally gobsmacked. So was everyone
else. The other kids on the FHK's team all
grumbled and groaned.

I walked towards them in a trance. I heard
Renfrew say something behind me. It might
have been, 'Watch out.'

'You go in goal, fatty,' said someone. I don't
really like going in goal, but I was chuffed
just to be playing, so I didn't mind.

The truth is, I did quite a good job –
I filled most of the goal and just let the balls
bounce off me. I didn't let a single one in,
and at the end we were winning 7–0.
The FHK clapped me on the back and
said, 'Well done, Donut.'

Pretty amazing, really.

I celebrated on the way home by getting
the holy trinity from Mr Alexis: a plain chocolate
donut, a milk chocolate donut and a white
chocolate donut.

It's funny. I was looking back over the donuts I've eaten, trying to work out if I eat more when I've had a rotten day. I think I usually do. But then I also eat more if I've had a really good day (like today). And then there's the whole mysterious factor of availability, which is all to do with whether I've got enough money, if the donuts have sold out, if I've been grounded, etc. etc.

So I reckon it's quite a tricky equation. And like all tricky equations, I've found it's best just not to think about it.

So, **DONUT COUNT:**

Wednesday 4 October

Played footie again at break. Only let in
one goal. The score so far this week is 12–1.
Suddenly everyone likes me!

Renfrew and Spam and Corky are a bit weird
about it, but they'll have to learn to live with my
new-found celebrity.

I haven't even thought about Doc Morlock's
poo for a couple of days. Oh, but now I have . . .

My mum talked to me tonight. Not the usual haveyoudoneyourhomeworkeatupyour spinachwillyoubrushyourteeth kind of talk, but a different sort. A new sort. I was actually trying to watch the telly, so it was slightly annoying. It went like this:

Mum: Those pictures you saw the other day.

Me: Yeah?

Mum: I want to explain about them.

Me: OK.

Mum: This is important, and it's difficult for me to talk about, so I'd appreciate it if you listened.

Me: Yeah. What?

Mum: I want to explain about them.

Me: OK. About what?

Mum: The pictures. About the girl in

them. About me. The thing is, when I was about eleven, I began to have a . . . difficult relationship with food.

Me: Oh.

Mum: I began to eat too much. And then I'd . . . well, I'd go for a while without eating anything.

Me: Oh.

Mum: And it just wasn't healthy.

Me: Oh.

Mum: And I became quite ill.

Me: Sorry, what were you saying?

[At this point Mum got up and turned the telly off. Doh!]

Mum: Look, what I'm saying is that I went through a very bad time, and I don't want you to go through it. It's why I want to get you eating healthily from an early age. It's why I don't want you to be . . .

Me: Fat.

Mum: Yes, fat.

Me: [After a few seconds of thinking time]
Mum?

Mum: Yes?

Me: How come you stopped being, you
know, fat?

Mum: Well, I suppose it was your dad.

Me: Dad? How?

Mum: He, er, loved me.

Me: *Muuuum* . . .

Mum: Well, you asked me. He loved me and
didn't care what I looked like, so I stopped being
quite so mixed up. And the strange thing is that
when I stopped being, well, a bit mad, then I
slimmed down. And of course there's the yoga.

Me: Mum?

Mum: Yes?

Me: Can we put the telly on again?

Then there was a double flush from the loo and my dad appeared. When he sat on the sofa my mum went and sat next to him and held his hand. I got out of there pretty quick in case they started snogging.

After that, I needed a donut!

DONUT COUNT:

Thursday 5 October

The guys are definitely getting jealous about my participation in the Big Match.

'They're just making fun of you, you know,' Renfrew said, not really looking at me. It was at the beginning of break, before the game had got going again.

'How do you know?' I replied, a bit grumpily.

'Because why else would they let you play?'

'Anyone can play who wants to. That's the rule. You could play if you wanted.'

'Yeah, sure.'

'No need to be sarcastic.'

'But why do you think they asked you to play?'

'I'm good in goal,' I said, a bit offended if truth be told.

'B-b-b-b-b b-b-h-h-h-h-h-h,' said Corky.

Spam didn't say anything.

Because of all that I was a bit distracted in the game, and I let three goals in. No one clapped me on the back, but Steerforth gave me a little smile.

A couple of plain donuts today.

I was thinking that maybe I could have a

donut fast for the two days before the poo test. That would be long enough for the donuts to get out of my system, wouldn't it?

DONUT COUNT:

Friday 6 October

It couldn't last.

Nothing good ever does.

Today I finally got to play out of goal in the
Big Match. It was the FHK's idea. I was trudging
towards the goal when he said, 'You can play
up front today, Donut.' Everyone groaned, but
he was the boss and they were all used to doing
what he said.

The game got going and no one passed
the ball to me, but I ran around as best I could

and even made a couple of tackles.

And then, it seemed I had my chance for glory. A couple of kids crashed into each other and the ball rolled free to me, not far from their goal. There was just the keeper to beat. I ran closer. I pulled back my foot. I was going to hit a rocket. It was going to win us the match. I was going to be famous. I saw how it would all happen. My new friends would all cluster around me. I'd make sure that Renfrew, Spam and Corky were included. I'd tell my dad all about it. It was going to be awesome. It was going to be epic.

I pulled the trigger. I swung my foot. It was a good swing. You could hear my foot whistle through the air like a peregrine falcon in its killing dive.

But just as I let fly I sensed movement to my

side, and the microsecond that I made contact
with the ball I felt a gentle nudge. In most
situations – walking down the school corridor
or whatever – I would barely have noticed it.
But at this precise moment it had a series of
catastrophic effects. It would have been better
if I'd just plain missed the ball, but I didn't. The
outside of my foot clipped the edge of the ball
and sent it in a spinning, slicing arc, metres wide
of the goal. I sensed that it was aiming straight
for a group of girls chattering together, the way
girls do. But I didn't have time to concentrate
on the path of the ball, because I was off-balance
and steaming at full speed towards another
group of kids.

A group of big kids.

Everything slowed down. I saw with amazing
clarity the faces of the kids I was heading

towards. They were prefects. Some of them were the prefects I'd met on my very first morning. The mean prefects. One of them was the really mean prefect – the one called, I remembered, Ivan. I saw him first look up, blankly, at the human missile heading his way. Then his face changed. Puzzlement. Anger. Finally fear. The other prefects were diving out of the way, but he seemed frozen. I tried to stop, but I was moving too fast. The brakes were on but I was sliding. I ducked my head. At the same time I saw, over to the side, the ball smash into the face of one of the girls.

Tamara Bello.

And then my head crunched right into the nuts of the nastiest prefect in the whole school.

I heard a sound like a dying moose and felt the hot breath of the prefect on the back of my

neck. At the same moment I heard an outraged
shriek from Tamara. It was the nearest thing to
an uncool sound she'd ever uttered.

Then I was lying on top of the prefect.

I'll relate what happened next as swiftly as I can. I was a bit dazed from the collision and so some of this I had to piece together from the testimonies of Renfrew and Spam who were watching with horrified fascination.

First, Ivan shoved me off him, and then did some rolling around in agony. The other prefects were caught between wanting to laugh and trying to look sympathetic. Then Ivan got up, still bent over, cupping his injured parts in his hands. He issued some instructions. The other prefects picked me up and carried me over to one of the big metal wheelie bins outside the school kitchens. They then proceeded to remove my trousers and throw me into the bin, where I landed on yesterday's rotten, stinking, festering scraps and scrapings. It

smelled pretty bad in there, like a tramp had
vomited into his own underpants and left
them there for me.

I looked up over the rim of the bin in time
to see Ivan the Terrible throw my trousers
out into the middle of the playground, where
a reasonable crowd had gathered. I then saw
Tamara walk over to them (my trousers, I mean).
She bent and picked them up with two fingers,
like they were radioactive or something. Then
she walked over to a big puddle and dropped
my trousers into it. Finally she stepped on the
trousers and did an amusing little dance, rubbing
them into the dirty water.

This was all accompanied by the usual
laughter, jeering, insults, etc. Quite a few kids
came over and banged on the side of the metal
bin as if it were a giant drum.

The bell went for the end of break and the kids all went in. When it had all died down Renfrew brought my trousers over to me and I put them on inside the bin.

For the rest of the day I was wet, stinky, depressed and surrounded by a quarantine zone that not even my friends dared to pass through.

To add insult to injury, I got a right old telling-off from Mum about the state of my uniform when I got in. I exchanged a look with Dad, who came briefly out of the toilet. I think he understood what had happened. I guess in his time he was probably dumped in the bin more than once.

Couldn't get any donuts today, even though it was my Hour of Greatest Need. My money must have fallen out in the bottom of the giant bin.

DONUT COUNT:

NO donuts

Saturday 7 October

After yesterday I needed a good day, and I had
one. Went swimming again with Dad. We didn't
take the girls this time. We've decided it should
be a guy thing we do together. It's good exercise
for me and it gets him out of the toilet.

We had sushi again afterwards, and because
the girls weren't there we could talk about
proper boy stuff without them pulling faces
like they were being tortured by the Spanish
Inquisition, although sometimes I think that Ella

would quite like to have lived in the days
of torture chambers, dungeons, thumb-screws
etc. etc.

So what we talked about was whether it
was better to have machine guns or cannons
on a fighter plane. Naturally enough, our case
study was the Battle of Britain and whether
the eight machine guns of the Hurricanes
and Spitfires were better than the two 20mm
cannons and four machine guns on the
Messerschmitt BF 109. It was actually quite
a close call. A single cannon shell could blow
a Spitfire out of the sky, whereas the British
planes needed to really hammer the evil Nazis
with their machine guns to shoot them down.
However, my dad said that the British pilots
weren't that well trained and the machine
guns sort of sprayed out bullets in a wide

pattern, which meant that they had a much better chance of hitting the target. It was a different matter when it came to shooting down bombers, such as the Heinkel He 111, Dornier Do 17 and Junkers Ju 88. Cannons would then have been very useful indeed.

So, that's the good bit of the conversation we had. And then my dad said something a bit strange.

'Dermot,' he said, looking at me.

'Yeah?'

'I'm glad we've had this talk now.'

'Why?'

'Because in a year, maybe two, you won't

want to talk about this sort of thing. Not with me, anyway.'

'Dad, of course I will! I love talking about guns and planes.'

'No, listen to me, Dermot. You'll be thinking about different stuff then. You know, girls and things . . .'

'Dad!'

'No, let me finish. I don't mind. In fact, I'll be pleased. It's natural. It's good. I'm just saying that these moments are important. I want us to remember them.'

'But you still like talking about this kind of thing, Dad.'

'Maybe I shouldn't. Maybe I never grew up properly. Maybe . . .'

'Shut up, Dad,' I said, and gave him a hug,

which was a bit awkward because there was all the sushi mess on the table.

It was all pretty embarrassing, but sort of nice as well.

Been giving much thought to Doc Morlock's poo sample. Think I may have hit on something ...

DONUT COUNT:

Sunday 8 October

Ruby's such a selfish cow. There's this pink
plastic beaker that she's had since she was two
or something. She used to have her milk out
of it, then her juice, now probably pink gin or
whatever it is that thirteen-year-old girls drink.
It is shaped roughly like a bear. It has pictures
of teddy bears on the outside. The teddy bears
are having, as you've probably guessed, a picnic.
As part of the picnic, the younger bears are
drinking. If you look carefully you can see that

they are drinking out of little pink beakers.
The little pink beakers have pictures on them.
Pictures of bears drinking out of beakers.
Which in turn have pictures of bears drinking
out of beakers. If you spend too long thinking
about it you go mad. Which maybe explains
why Ruby is like she is . . .

Anyway, this beaker always used to fascinate
and horrify me, sort of sucking me into its
world of bears-within-bears. So, when I was
looking for something a bit *bigger* to use for
collecting the sample for Doc Morlock I
thought, well . . .

The trouble was that I was knocking on
the toilet door, telling Dad to hurry up, when
Ruby came by and saw what I was carrying.

'What are you doing with Beaky?' she yelled.

'Nothing,' I replied, obviously.

'Then why are you holding him? Why are you taking him into the toilet? What the heck are you planning?'

Before I had the chance to answer she snatched at the thing. I didn't just want to give in to her, so we had a bit of a wrestling match, which she was winning because she's bigger than me and girls fight dirty – biting, gouging, scratching, hair-pulling, etc. etc. Then Dad came out of the toilet and Mum came up the stairs, and I had to explain what was going on. I probably should have lied about it, said that I was just using the bear to get a drink of water, but in the end I lost my temper and yelled out, 'I was going to dump in your Beaky!'

So that's why I'm up here now, alone, with no donuts.

And I still haven't solved the Great Poo
Problem. And time is running out.

DONUT COUNT:

Monday 9 October

Mr Wells announced today that Year Seven are
going on a day trip to Chimpsters Zoo next
week, as a treat before half term. Mr Wells
was probably expecting a big cheer. What he
got was a sort of groan.

Chimpsters isn't the world's greatest zoo. It
doesn't have any decent rides, just a little train
that puffs its way around, plus a climbing frame
and some tyres for swings. The animals aren't that
amazing either. They have some scabby-looking

lions, some scabbier-looking hyenas, a couple
of zebras, a camel or two, a pygmy hippo, some
meerkats and quite a few other insignificant
things I can't remember the names of.

It's most famous for its colony of chimpanzees,
after which the place got named. But even with
the chimps there's a problem. The boss chimp,
a big bruiser called Samson, has a particularly
dirty habit which can make going to look at
the chimps a messy business. I found out about
Samson's nasty habit a couple of years ago when
our family visited. I don't want to say exactly what
Samson's dirty habit is right now, but let's just say
that Ruby had to go straight home to shower, and
Dad burned her pink dress in the garden.

At break I told Renfrew about this.

'She was probably staring at him in the eye,'
he said. 'They don't like that. Especially the

big males. It's a threat in Chimp language. You might as well go up to them and say, "Anyone fancy a fight?"'

Spam joined in. 'I saw a clip on YouTube of a kid getting his arm ripped off by a chimp at some zoo in Germany. They sewed it back on again afterwards, so it all ended happily, except that in all the excitement they sewed it on the wrong way round so now he can't clap properly. But I reckon that's probably worth it for the brilliant story you'd get out of it.'

'B-b-b-b-b-b-b-h-h-h-h-h-h-h,' said Corky, and I think I know what he meant.

Doc Morlock tomorrow, so no donuts today.

DONUT COUNT:

NO
donuts

Tuesday 10 October

The thing about falling from a great height is that you never know when you reach the bottom because when you do you're just a splat of strawberry jam that can't know anything.

Today was poo day.

At least I'd worked out a way of getting a sample.

In the end I used one of my dad's old spectacle cases. He's got loads of them because he keeps losing his glasses, and every time he buys a new pair he gets a swanky new case. I won't go into details. I don't mean the details of how Dad keeps losing his glasses. I mean, the details of how I got the poo into the glasses case. Because, frankly, that would be gross. Just accept the fact that where once there was an empty glasses case, now there was a glasses case with a poo in it.

I got the bus across town to the clinic. Although it shut with a satisfying snap, the glasses case wasn't completely airtight. It meant that a bit of a smell leaked out. An old lady came and sat next to me on the bus, but she didn't stay very long. She gave me a look that was about ten per cent pity and ninety per cent horror. I thought about trying to explain but, well, how could I? What was I supposed to say?

'Er, I haven't pooped my pants or anything . . . I've

just got some poo in this glasses case which I'm taking
to a fake lady doctor who is going to look at it and see
if I've been eating too many donuts.'

I was thinking that this may be a new low for
me. But not the bottom. I was still falling.

I hadn't gone splat yet.

Half an hour later I was sitting in the waiting
room in the health centre where Doc Morlock
has her clinic. I had the glasses case on my lap. I
was reading Alan Moore's mighty *The Watchmen*
– probably the greatest graphic novel ever
penned.

It was pretty hot and stuffy in the waiting
room. Strangely, all the other people were
crammed in the opposite corner to me. Well, not
strangely. It was because of the foul reek of poo
surrounding me like a cloud of poison gas.

I sensed someone else come in. I looked up.

It was Tamara Bello.

I was still falling. I waited for the splat.

Tamara looked for somewhere to sit. She saw the seat next to me and headed for it. The second before she sat down she recognized me.

'You,' she said, without any surprise or emotion in her voice.

I hadn't had a chance yet to say sorry about booting the ball in her face. I tried now. 'I'm really sorry about—'

'What's that stink?'

I'd forgotten about the poo in the glasses case. 'It's . . . er . . . this place always pongs. All these sick people. They, er, probably have diarrhoea. Or, er, cholera. Dysentery. Wind.'

Smooth, eh?

Tutting, Tamara sat down. 'What are you

reading a comic for?' she said, before I had time to finish my apology.

'It's not a comic – it's the greatest—'

'I'm sorry,' she interrupted.

'Sorry . . . ? What for?'

'Throwing your trousers in the puddle.'

Well, *that* was unexpected.

'Oh. I'm sorry I kicked the ball in your face. It was an accident.'

'No, it wasn't.'

'But really, I didn't mean to—'

'I know *you* didn't mean to do anything. You're harmless.'

I was completely lost. 'What are you talking about?'

'It was *him*. He pushed you just as you were about to kick the ball.'

'Who?'

'Don't be such a dummy. Steerforth. Who else?'

'But he was on my side.'

'He isn't on anyone's side except his own.'

I replayed the events in my head. Could it have been Steerforth, the FHK, who nudged me as I tried to score? Could he really have planned the whole thing? Was that the only reason he had let me play in the Big Match? He'd have to be an evil genius. It was too much for my poor brain to take in.

'How do you know so much about him?'

Another big tut from Tamara. 'He's my cousin.'

'Oh.' This was all too heavy for me. I didn't know what to say. So I changed the subject. 'What are you here for?'

Tamara looked me right in the eye. 'Verrucas. You?'

'Oh ...' I couldn't help but look down at the spectacle case. Her eyes followed mine. Her cute nose wrinkled.

'Didn't know you wore glasses,' she said.

'Let's see . . . ?' She reached out to take them.

The ground was rushing towards me.

I imagined her face. The horror. Imagined what she would say at school. The glasses case. The poo. The freak.

This was it.

The splat was coming.

'Dermot, come in please.'

I looked up to see Doc Morlock standing outside her door. For one second I felt pure love for the nasty old prune, with her face looking like an angry handbag.

'Sorry, got to, er, go.'

I followed Doc Morlock, feeling both saved and doomed.

Can't write any more today. Will have to finish the story tomorrow.

Wednesday 11 October

OK, got my strength back (he said, wiping donut crumbs from his mouth). What happened next was this:

'How have you been?' asked Doc Morlock when I was sitting down. The vulture was back, getting ready to stick its head into that dead wildebeest's body.

'OK.'

'Everything all right at school?' The vulture's claws were on the carcass.

'Yeah.'

'And how's the diet coming along? You've been good?' The baldy head and the hooked beak were in.

'Not too bad.'

'You have the sample?' And out comes some juicy bit of meat.

'Yeah, it's, er . . .' I held out the glasses case.

'Why would I want your glasses?'

'No, it's . . . you know . . . in there.'

Somehow her face became even more vulturial, if that's a word.

'Why didn't you use the sample container I gave you?'

'It was too small. I couldn't . . . I mean, my aim . . . I mean, it . . .'

'Didn't you read the instructions?'

Had there been some instructions? Maybe

there had been a piece of paper, but I'd just chucked it away. Do I look like the kind of kid who needs to be told how to go to the toilet?

'You were supposed,' continued the evil doc, 'to use the spatula to take a small sample and put it in the container.'

'Oh, sorry.'

'Never mind, give it here.'

I passed her the case and Doc Morlock put it in a clear plastic envelope and stood up.

'Wait here while I go and analyse this in the lab,' she said, and left the room.

I felt like a man on trial for his life, waiting for the jury to return their verdict. Suddenly the clock began to tick very loudly. A fly buzzed in the window, sounding like a jet plane taking off.

Five minutes later the doc was back. She walked silently up to the stool chart. The stick was in her hand. She pointed to Type 2.

'This is where we are, Dermot. I found traces of partially digested refined carbohydrates.'

'Eh?'

'Sugar, Dermot, sugar. And there was evidence of the kind of food dyes they put in icing. The sort of icing that covers . . . need I say it, Dermot?'

I shook my head. Already I was eating gruel at Camp Fatso.

'However . . . I did note that there were some signs of a reasonable intake of fruit and vegetables, and the sugar levels were just within acceptable levels.'

I wanted to let out a yowl of delight. But Doc Morlock was not done yet.

'Which is why I am prepared to give you one last chance, Dermot. If, on your next visit, I find

a magnificent example of a Type Three or
Four stool, with no traces of donut whatsoever,
then . . . then we'll see.'

I was drinking in the last-chance saloon. They
didn't serve donuts.

DONUT COUNT:

Thursday 12 October

I'd been planning my revenge which, I'm told, is a dish best served cold. Just like a donut. Actually, I suppose your *ideal* donut is served at blood temperature. No one really wants a *cold* donut, like out of the fridge or something. That would be plain wrong. But then so would a *hot* donut. Wouldn't it?

Suddenly I'm not so sure. In fact, I'm going to try it. Back in a minute.

Well, that was interesting, if you find near-death experiences interesting, that is. Sneaked into the kitchen while Mum was watching telly and Dad was in the toilet. Put a jam donut in the microwave – just for five seconds. Ping. Nibbled it. Quite nice, but thought it needed a few more seconds. Gave it another thirty. Ping. Bit it. The spongy bit of the donut was fine, but the jam had turned into boiling lava. It squirted its deadliness right into my mouth. I spat it out, but not before it had stripped the skin from the inside of my mouth, the way pizza cheese does when it's too hot. I let out a strangled scream and gulped cold water straight from the tap.

This was undoubtedly the worst donut experience of my life, if you don't count the curried donut Mr Alexis made me try as part of the Donuts of the World promotion.

Dad came in and helped me tidy up before

Mum saw what was going on.

'I thought you, er, you know, stopped with the donuts.'

'I've cut right down, Dad.'

'OK, because, well . . . Camp Fatso. That would be a fiasco, and neither of us want that, do we?'

'No, Dad.'

We both looked at the door through to the living room. We both knew that what we wanted didn't matter. If Mum wanted it, then it was going to happen.

Sorry, I was talking about revenge, wasn't I? Against the FHK. Everything rubbish that had happened to me since I went to secondary school was down to him. He'd planned it all. Why? Because I was a bit of a fatty.

It wasn't fair.

Well, he's going to pay for it. All I need is a nice, evil plan.

The trouble is, I'm useless at thinking up evil plans. It's because I'm one of the goodies. Pity.

DONUT COUNT:

Friday 13 October

I had an insight into what awaits me in Camp
Fatso. I should have known I was in for it after
getting on the wrong side of Mr Fricker ages
ago when I called him a cyborg. Some people
carry a grudge. Some people don't. Mr Fricker,
it turns out, does. Carries it, that is, up on top of
his head where everyone can see it, like the way
ladies in Africa carry water jars.

The screaming began when we took too long
to get changed into our PE kits. There was the

sinister quiet bit while he told us that we were going to be running for miles through the mud, and then lots more screaming incredibly loudly as we ran along. This was only the boys. The girls got to do netball with nice Miss Gunasekara.

Suddenly netball seemed like the best sport ever invented. Suddenly a small part of me slightly sort of wanted to be a girl.

NOTE TO SELF: NEVER SAY OR THINK ANYTHING LIKE THIS EVER AGAIN.

Of course, the whole thing was a nightmare for me. I'm not very good at running, so I was

at the back the whole time with Mr Fricker
jogging beside me, screaming directly into my
face. Renfrew and Spam kept me company for
a while, but Corky was up at the front, way
ahead. Turns out he's as fast as a greased rocket.
But soon even Renfrew and Spam were out
of sight, because Mr Fricker kept screaming,

'You're not trying, boy! Down on that fat gut and give me five press-ups!' which slowed me down even more, as you'd expect. Five press-ups may not sound very much, but it's pretty rubbish when you have to do them in the mud with an authentic loony screaming at you, and when you're shattered anyway because of all the running you've been doing.

Luckily Fricker only had his normal artificial hands on — if he'd had the electric prod or lightsaber attachments things would have been even worse. As it was, it was exactly like being in hell and having your own personal tormenter.

We began by running twice round the rugby pitch, then we ran along the side of the canal, then over a bridge, then back down the other side of the canal, then across a field then, well, then I got confused and had no idea at all where I was going.

By the time we'd got back to the rugby pitch I was completely covered in mud and my lungs were screaming for air and my legs were made of wet jelly. The one good thing was that I'd gone deaf so I couldn't hear Fricker screaming any more. All the other kids were sitting at the end of the field waiting for us. I sat down to join them, but Fricker screamed: 'Get up, boy! Twice more round the pitch, double speed!'

By the time I'd got back to the gym the others had all changed and left, even my friends.

I was so tired I fell asleep on the bus home and missed my stop and had to walk back.

Dinner was another showcase for the

technique of removing the flavour from food by the physical process of boiling: boiled fish with boiled potatoes and boiled carrots. Dessert was boiled plums.

I think I'd rather have eaten plain boils.

DONUT COUNT:

NO
donuts

Saturday 14 October

Ping.

I've had my light bulb moment. An idea.
A genuine idea. It came to me while I was
swimming. It may be the best idea since Ug first
watched a round stone roll down a hill as he was
dragging his wheel-less cart along, and invented
bowling.

Or it may be rubbish. The trouble is, it's
got lots of pieces which have to fit together
perfectly, or the whole thing collapses, with

me looking worse than ever.

I need to think it through carefully. And for that my brain needs food. The right food.

You know what I'm saying.

DONUT COUNT:

Sunday 15 October

Still working on my brilliant plan. I've drawn it all out on a big piece of paper. I filled it up and used every single colour of Ruby's felt tips.

Oh yeah, there was a bit of a fuss about that – she's been nervous about me using her stuff ever since the incident with Beaky. She scribbled all over my diagram, ruining it, so I said that I was going to tell Jim that she fancied him. That shut Ruby up, and she ran out of the room, which was a bit unexpected.

Maybe she does fancy him . . . ?

Anyway, tomorrow I put this plan into operation. Really quite excited.

DONUT COUNT:

NO donuts

Monday 16 October

At lunch time today, there was a 'scene' in the dining hall. I'm afraid I was in it.

It must have looked really bad.

We were sitting at our usual table staring in dismay at the steamed liver and mashed turnips (or maybe steamed turnips and mashed liver). Renfrew had been sulking all day. Everyone had mentioned it. But if you asked him, 'What's up, Renfrew?' he'd just say, 'Nothing,' in a sort of grumpy snarl.

Then it all kicked off. I was telling the guys about how Jim's dad was going to take us paintballing for Jim's birthday, when Renfrew suddenly threw down his knife and fork with a crash, and stood up.

'I'm sick of you going on about your brilliant mates at home. If you think they're so great, why don't you clear off to *their* school? You're so thick you'd probably fit right in.'

Loads of people were watching this, their mouths hanging open. No one had ever heard Renfrew shout before.

I said, 'Sit down, Renfrew, you idiot,' but he just stormed straight out of the hall, the big drama queen.

Well, *little* drama queen, really.

'What was all that about?' said Spam, looking upset.

I shrugged. 'Dunno.'

'B-b-b-h-h-h,' said Corky.

Little did any of them know that my brilliant plan had begun. Well, one person knew. The others would be informed only when it was strictly necessary.

Muwhahaha!

(That was meant to be an evil laugh, by the way, not the sound of me puking up the boiled liver.)

DONUT COUNT:

(I've decided to try to stick to one donut per day, just in case something goes wrong with my scheme.)

Tuesday 17 October

It all came to a head the next day at break. By now word had got round that me and Renfrew had fallen out. Some kids were saying that we were going to have a fight. Others said that we were too wimpy and there's no way we'd get stuck in. But there was definitely that buzz in the air. It felt a bit weird.

Anyway, I was standing with Corky and Spam when Renfrew came up to me, sticking his chin out like he was hard or something.

'You're so fat, when you walk backwards you go "beep, beep, beep",' he said.

'Good one, Renfrew,' I replied. 'Shame you stole it off the internet. But it doesn't matter. I could lose weight if I wanted, but you'll always look like a rodent.'

Renfrew's face set hard. A crowd had gathered round. I could see the playground monitor, a woman called Mrs Smote who was a bit simple and wore wellington boots in all weathers, beginning to get agitated.

Then Renfrew tried to push me over. Renfrew probably weighs half what I do. He may as well have tried to push over a tree. Someone in the crowd laughed. And something else happened. Someone had moved behind Renfrew. It meant that when I gave Renfrew a really quite modest push, he fell

over the crouching figure of . . . Spam!

The oldest trick in the book, and still one of the finest.

The crowd loved it. I saw the smirking face of the FHK. I also saw the unsmiling face of Tamara Bello.

But then Mrs Smote arrived to see what was going on, so we all had to split.

I felt pretty bad about Renfrew this evening.

But then I had my one donut and felt better.

That's the power of the donut.

DONUT COUNT:

Wednesday 18 October

I was walking along the corridor on the way to Miss Michelet's French class when a strong arm threw me against the wall. I shut my eyes and got ready for a punch in the guts or a dead arm or whatever. Nothing happened, so I opened my eyes again.

It was Tamara Bello.

'Hello,' I said. 'How are your verrucas?' It wasn't until later that I thought that she might interpret that as a bit rude.

'I don't know why I'm doing this . . .'

'What, shoving me against the wall?'

'No, warning you.'

'Warning me? About what?'

Tamara tutted and rolled her eyes and generally gave the impression of someone who really wanted to be somewhere else.

'Right, so I saw your friend Renfrew talking to Steerforth this morning. Amanda Cunningham was standing close to them, and I asked her what they'd been talking about. We all know what a swine Steerforth is, and it seemed weird him talking to Renfrew . . . Anyway, she told me that Renfrew told Steerforth that he had a good plan for really destroying you at Chimpsters. Something to do with a ditch and some stinky water. And Steerforth said that he didn't want to get expelled, and Renfrew said he'd make it look like it was all your fault, and that Steerforth was only trying to help you. Anyway, it all sounded pretty sneaky, so I thought I'd tell you. But don't get thinking that I'm bothered, 'cos I'm not. Anyway, I thought Renfrew and you were supposed to be friends?'

'Yeah, well, we were. So what?'

She stared at me for a couple of seconds and then tossed her hair and walked off.

The school trip is tomorrow. The day after that I go to see Doc Morlock. And then, unless something very special happens, it's half term and Camp Fatso for me.

I've worked out my plan. There are several different bits, and they all have to come off or the whole thing will collapse. This is making me very nervous.

The only way to calm my nerves is with a

you-know-what. Nothing fancy, just a solid,
plain 100 per cent donut. Didn't enjoy it much.
Sort of stuck in my throat and I had to wash
it down with milk. I blame the thing with
Renfrew.

DONUT COUNT:

Thursday 19 October

Everyone was excited in the morning. We were
allowed to wear our own clothes, so I didn't
look like such a freak. I'm not saying I looked
good – I just had my jeans and a normal, non-
embarrassing shirt and a zip-up jacket – but
at least I didn't look like a plum about to go
nuclear. Spam was wearing a yellow jumper
and a pair of trousers that were, I suppose, light
brown, but which also looked a bit yellowy.
Together it made him look like a giant streak

of snot fired out of a footballer's nose. Corky was wearing tracky bottoms and a Stoke City football top. He doesn't support Stoke City. *Nobody* supports Stoke City. Life is full of mysteries.

Renfrew had forgotten that you could wear your own clothes and had turned up in his school uniform, which made him look like a total loser.

'You look like a total loser,' I said to him, in front of everyone.

He shot me back a look of pure venom. It actually had more impact than the shove he'd given me the other day, and I took a step back.

'Well, that's enough of that, Dermot,' said Mr Wells.

There were three coaches taking us to

Chimpsters, and the classes all got mixed up.

Some of the tough sporty kids from Newman sat at the back of our coach, and some brainiacs from Campion sat at the front. That left me and Corky and Spam in the middle, which was OK.

After ten minutes, Mr Wells came and sat near us. He leaned over and said: 'Everything all right with you, Dermot?'

'Yeah, sir, fine.'

'It's just that I noticed that you and Renfrew don't seem to be getting on very well ...'

I shrugged and looked out of the window. We were going past a garage. Unleaded petrol cost 121.1p per litre, which I thought was a pretty odd price for anything. I mean, if you bought exactly one litre, you'd have to pay one pound twenty-one, plus one tenth of a penny. Stoopid. I thought Mr Wells was going to ask some more questions, and I made up some good answers as the stoopid garage zoomed backwards, but he just went off to sit with Miss Brotherton who everyone says he fancies.

We reached Chimpsters and all piled out of the coach. The teachers with us were Mr Wells, Miss Brotherton, Mr Braintree and the dreaded Mr Fricker.

Mr Wells tried to get everyone to calm down, but nobody did until Mr Fricker screamed at us, which freaked out a couple of nearby zebras and a camel.

I saw Renfrew standing with the FHK and his cronies. He looked at me furtively.

Or was it guiltily?

Then the fun started. We were divided up into groups, each one with a teacher in charge.

Ours was, you've guessed it, Mr Psycho Fricker.
The groups were mixed up, but luckily I had
Spam and Corky in mine. There was also snooty
Tamara Bello, plus various Campions, Xaviers
and Newmans.

'He's probably come to wreak revenge on
the leopard that got his hands,' whispered Spam,
pointing at Fricker.

He just had on his normal everyday
mechanical hands rather than any of his special
attachments. Maybe he had a tranquillizer
dart attachment in his bag for escaped–animal
emergencies.

Mr Fricker handed out work sheets full of
questions that we had to answer. Each group had
the questions in a different order so we didn't all
visit the same animals at the same time.

Our first question was: 'How many toes does

a pygmy hippo have?' So we headed for the pygmy hippo pen to check it out.

The pygmy hippo, it turns out, has four toes on each foot, making sixteen all together. Cute little fellow.

'The proper, full-sized hippos kill more people in Africa than lions do,' said Spam cheerily.

'Yeah, but you'd have to be some sort of midget to be killed by one of those things,' I replied.

'But they have pygmy people in Africa, don't they?' Spam continued, oddly reluctant to let the subject lie. 'I bet they get regularly massacred by pygmy hippos.'

I had to agree that it was possible.

'B-b-b-b-b-b-b-h-h-h-h-h-h-h,' said Corky.

After the hippo, the next question was: 'How

can you tell a jaguar from a leopard?' I knew
the answer to this already, but we still went to
the jaguar enclosure and then to the leopard
enclosure, which were both in the 'Big Cats'
part of the zoo.

We were standing there staring at the leopard's
ear, which was the only bit of it we could
see, when Mr Fricker loomed up. He hadn't
screamed for ages, so I thought that's what he'd
come over to do. He was staring quite hard at
the leopard's ear. Spam and Corky both gave me
significant looks. Suddenly the leopard-theory of
how Mr Fricker lost his hands started to seem a
lot less far-fetched.

Then Mr Fricker spoke. 'How can a leopard
change its spots?'

'Pardon, sir?' I said, a bit mystified.

'I said, how can a leopard change its spots?'

'I think it's a joke,' whispered Spam.

'I don't know, sir,' I said.

'When it gets tired of one spot, it just moves to another.'

There was a moment's silence. It was really quite awkward. Then Corky started to laugh. Maybe it was just supposed to be a quick 'Ha!' but because of his stammer it went 'H-h-h-h-h-h-h-h-h-h-h-h-ha.'

Mr Fricker looked at Corky, possibly checking to make sure he wasn't laughing sarcastically, but Corky was wiping tears from his eyes, so Fricker seemed happy enough.

The next question was: 'Find your closest relation.'

Well, that was easy. They obviously didn't mean Mum, Dad, Ruby or Ella.

To the chimps we went.

We got there just as another group was leaving. That group included my former friend Renfrew and his new friend, the FHK. The FHK was wearing a long black coat that almost looked like a cloak. Quite cool, actually. Ella would have loved it.

I surveyed the chimpanzee enclosure from a safe distance. There were about fifteen chimps generally lazing around the place. Some were lying over branches, their arms and legs dangling. Some were squatting against the wall, looking like hooligans. A few more were in the indoors part of their enclosure, and you could see them sitting in piles of straw, smoking cigarettes, drinking beer and watching telly. Not really, but they did look a bit like that.

And then I saw the one I was looking for. He was twice the size of the other chimps. His face wore an expression of contempt, combined with a barely controlled rage.

He was one angry chimp.

He was the boss.

He was the one they call Samson.

I looked at Corky and Spam, and nodded. It was time to put into operation everything we had planned. The next few minutes were going to mean disaster or triumph.

I moved forward to a spot right in front of the evil Samson. He was below me, but only about ten metres away. I was quite safe from physical attack because of the moat. The moat stank. It was probably half full of chimp poo.

Samson looked at me. His eyes were black and full of hatred. You could almost imagine what he was thinking.

Something like:

How dare these bald pink weaklings keep me
here. I should be swinging through the jungle, chasing
monkeys, getting cosy with loads of lady chimps, in
fact generally doing whatever chimp stuff I want to do.
But instead I'm in this rubbish enclosure, with this
blimp staring at me. Me, the mighty Samson, King of
all the Chimps. Well, if we were in the jungle I would

tear your arms off and suck your lungs out through the
holes. Hang on, just going to have a quick banana.

There was a banana on the floor next to
Samson. He picked it up without taking his
black eyes off me. Then he ate the banana
without even bothering to peel it.

Now, people go on about how brainy
chimpanzees are, but if that's true, how come
Samson never learned how to peel a banana, eh?

But that's not important now. I could feel the
rage building up in Samson. Feel the raw hatred
in his glance. He finished the banana. He flexed
his long hands – he was definitely imagining
how nice it would be to tear my arms off. I
stared right back, trying hard not to blink.

Then Samson moved even closer, right up to
the edge of the moat. I could smell him, I really
could. He smelled like my dad in the morning:

fusty and hot and a bit eggy.

He sat for a moment longer, thinking (Samson, I mean, not my dad). Then he lifted up his chimpy bottom, and slipped his hand underneath. He closed one eye. It wasn't a wink. Humans are the only animals capable of winking.* He was concentrating.

Things then happened quickly. I sensed a movement behind me. Mr Fricker coming to drag me back from the edge? I hoped not. I sincerely hoped not. For then, with a flurry and a fizz, Samson stood and hurled a greeny-brown boomerang of chimp-poo at me.

* I don't actually 100% know if this is true. There might be a shrimp or mole or something that can wink, but I sort of doubt it. And if I'm right, then I've just invented a really good scientific theory, which will probably make me famous.

And now that the moment had come, everything slowed down, just as it's supposed to do when you're about to die.

I saw the poop hurtling towards me. It spun majestically as it moved through the air. A small dollop flew off from one end, like a chunk of World War Two bomber shot off by an attacking fighter. But the rest of the fuselage was still hanging together, still flying, still heading directly for my face. Samson was one heck of a shot. It was going to land right in my mouth. I was going to be eating the old chimp-poo burger.

Samson was already celebrating, like a footballer who knew his penalty was heading for the top corner. His arms were in the air and he was beginning his victory *Whoooooooooooop!* The other chimps were running forward, ready to congratulate their leader. It was one in the eye for humanity! Centuries of oppression and torture were going to be put right.

And then I ducked.

And as I ducked, I turned.

I saw behind me the astonished expression of Steerforth, the Floppy-Haired Kid. His hands were out, ready to give me a shove in the back. I saw him glance down at me, and then up again.

His eyes narrowed, and then a look of horror came over his face.

But only for about, I'd say, one hundredth of a second. Because then the poop smacked into his chops with a sound like a bare buttock being hit with a cricket bat.

The splat had landed!

Corky and Spam and Renfrew were there, killing themselves laughing. In fact, Spam

and Renfrew were laughing so much they just couldn't speak. Corky, however, took a step forward, and said, in a voice as clear as a glass of sparkling mineral water:

'Serves you right, you F-f-f-f-floppy-Haired K-k-k-k-k-k-k-kid!'

OK, OK, I know you've guessed it. The plan wasn't actually that complicated, but it wasn't bad for a bunch of twelve-year-olds.

This is how it worked: Renfrew and me only pretended to have fallen out. Renfrew's part was to act like he wanted to get me back for all the mean things I'd done to him, so he went and told the FHK to push me into the moat, and then help drag me out, acting like he'd saved me. Spam and Corky had gone and distracted Mr Fricker by asking him about his various hand-attachments.

Of course, the whole beautiful mechanism depended on Samson doing his thing with the poop. But, like I said, he was famous for it, and I guessed that by giving him the eye good and proper, he'd deliver the goods.

The rest was down to good ducking – and you don't live for twelve years with my sisters without getting good at ducking!

Anyway, loads of kids saw Steerforth get the chimp-poo in the gob. Even his usual cronies and bum-kissers were laughing at him. Samson and the other chimps were all going, well, ape down in the enclosure, running around and whooping and generally making merry.

Steerforth tried to wipe the muck off, but he just smeared it across his face, which was glowing bright red. He stared at me, a look of incandescent rage distorting his usually super-cool face. He raised his hand, pointing a finger at me. His mouth began to form words, but nothing came out. Then he clenched his fist. I thought I might have to do some more ducking, but then a voice rang out.

'You lot! What's going on here?'

It was Mr Fricker, waving his mechanical hands.

Steerforth gave me one more evil glance, and then ran away to try to find a toilet to wash himself. We didn't see him for the rest of the day.

Tamara Bello witnessed it all, and even she showed off her lovely white teeth in a smile as big as Samson's banana.

And was that a wink? A WINK? From Tamara Bello? Maybe.

Anyway, me and Corky and Spam and Renfrew – good old Renfrew, whose task had been the hardest – had what can only be described as a group hug. It was the best feeling I'd had since . . . well, it was the best feeling I'd ever had.

But the defeat and humiliation of Steerforth was only half of the plan. The second half involved another of my dad's spectacle cases.

Enough for one day.

A donut? Tonight, of all nights, I really don't need 'em!

DONUT COUNT:

NO donuts

Friday 20 October

I was expecting something from Steerforth today.
I didn't know what. Perhaps some ingenious
humiliation, or just a brilliant put-down. Or
maybe an old-fashioned beating, his henchmen
holding my arms while he slapped my face
with a leather glove like a Gestapo officer in a
war film.

I didn't care. This morning at school I was a
hero. News of my triumph had obviously leaked
out. Well, it had leaked out because I'd told

anyone who would listen all about it, and so had Renfrew, Spam and Corky. Kids I didn't even know came up to me and said, 'Nice one.'

It happened at morning break. I was waiting for it, with the guys. I saw Steerforth get his posse together at the other end of the yard. Eight or nine of them. I checked out my gang:

Renfrew, his gerbil face set hard.

Spam, looking as ever like a decent breeze would snap him in half, but his eyes were steady.

Corky who, among all of us, was the one who would probably enjoy a bit of argy-bargy, the ancient schoolyard conversation between fists and faces.

I sensed that the whole school was watching. There weren't many fights at St Michael's – it wasn't that sort of school. But, if anything, that added to the excitement.

Five metres away, Steerforth stopped.

He stared.

I stared back.

Was there a slight tremor in my eyelid? There might have been.

And then came that huge, open, honest smile. A smile so dazzling it suddenly made the whole world seen less bright in comparison.

'Donut,' said Steerforth, his voice as rich and warm and friendly as a cup of hot chocolate with marshmallows floating in it. 'Donut, you're a genius. That was brilliant.'

And then he walked the rest of the way towards me, grabbed my hand and pumped it, never letting that smile dim for a second.

There was a sort of a cheer from the crowd of kids that had gathered – a release of tension, I suppose, along with a surge of admiration for very impressed. In all honesty, it's one of the finest human stools I've ever examined.'

'Great.'

'And on the basis of this, I shall tell your mother that there is no need for you to attend Camp Fatso.'

I let out a sigh. Angels sang in my head. The world seemed suddenly bright and beautiful.

'Just one thing, though, Dermot . . .'

Oh no. She'd seen through me. She'd been toying with me, the way a killer whale toys with a baby seal before biting its head off.

'You're eating an awful lot of bananas, Dermot.'

'Er, yeah, I like bananas. They've sort of taken the place of donuts in my life.'

'Fine, they're very good for potassium. But Dermot . . .'

'Yeah?'

'It's generally thought to be a good idea to peel them first.'

DONUT COUNT:

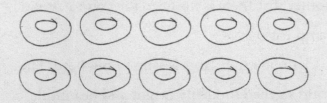

(But that was shared around between me, Renfrew, Corky, Spam and Jim who, even though he's not a donut fan, ate one to be sociable with my new friends.)

Acknowledgements

My thanks to the superb team at
Random House Children's Books:

Annie Eaton, Kelly Hurst,
Natalie Doherty, Sue Cook
and Lauren Bennett.

I took a pen out of my pocket and drew a pair of mean little eyes and a sharp nose and a cat's-bum mouth on one of the stools – Type 3, described as: *like a sausage, but with cracks on its surface.*

It now looked exactly like Doc Morlock.

I'd just sat down again when Doc Morlock came back into the consulting room. She looked puzzled. Perhaps a bit disappointed.

'Well, Dermot, I have to say I'm surprised.'

'Really?' I smiled. 'Why?'

'My analysis showed a complete absence of refined carbohydrates—'

'Sugar, I remember.'

'Quite, Dermot, sugar. Which indicates that you have not eaten any donuts. I also note that there is a very high fibre content. You've gone all the way from Type Two to Type Four. I'm really

Saturday 21 October

I'll paint you the scene. I'd delivered the latest sample to Doc Morlock. There was the usual grimacing, screwed-up, sucking-on-a-lemon face.

'I hope,' she said, 'that we can do better than last time.' But frankly, I doubt it. I've already called ahead to the commandant of Camp Fatso. Your bunk is ready. The gruel is warming.'

Once again she took my sample out of the room. I waited. I went over to the poo chart.

'What was all that about?' asked Renfrew.

'B-b-b-b-b-b-b-b-b-h-h-h-h-h-h-h-h-h-h,' said Corky.

'Not for the first time, Corky,' I said, 'you've hit the nail on the head.'

Anyway, that's still all to do with Part One of my plan which, although pretty cool, was not actually as important as Part Two. And whether or not that works, I'll find out tomorrow. If it doesn't, then my triumph over sly old Steerforth will count for nothing, as I will be on my way to the dreaded Camp Fatso for a week of ice-cold showers, cross-country runs, porridge and gruel.

DONUT COUNT:

a kid who could get a load of chimp-poo in the face and be able to laugh about it. Such panache! Such generosity of spirit!

Then Steerforth pulled me closer, and in a voice that came from some terrifying place, a place of utter blackness and evil – think Mordor, think the voice of Sauron himself – he said:

'I'm going to crush you, fatso. I'm going to make you wish you'd never come to this school. I'm going to make you wish, in fact, that you'd never been born. I'm going to destroy you and everyone you care about. Got that? Good.'

As he said it he pinched the hairs at the nape of my neck, twisted and yanked. It felt like a hornet sting. But I'd been expecting it, and I didn't flinch.

And then, with a final friendly pat on my shoulder, he was gone.